THE BOY WHO SAVED BASEBALL

JOHN H. RITTER

SCHOLASTIC INC.

New York Toronto London Auckland Sydney
Mexico City New Delhi Hong Kong Buenos Aires

IN ACKNOWLEDGEMENT

I owe deep thanks to my own all-star team, which includes fastballers Patty Ladd and Wilma Kelsey, curveballers Beth Brust and Jayne Haines, screwballers Tony Robles and Gayla Robles, baseball librarian Kent Goepfert, cyberphys-wiz Brian Ritter, along with my dream team, Mack the Finger and Louie the King, Blackjack Buck and a bird that sings. Also, deepest gratitude to my highly cognitive wife and mentor, Cheryl, as well as to my editor and personal Del Gato, Michael Green. And finally, *muchas gracias* to the heavy hitters in Mrs. Ritter's amazing class of 2002 at Explorer Elementary Charter School.

Much obliged,

JHR

ISBN 0-439-65305-3

12 11 10 9 8 7   5 6 7 8 9/0

Printed in the U.S.A.   40

First Scholastic printing, May 2004

Book design by Gunta Alexander. The text is set in Wilke.

This one is for my dad, Carl W. Ritter,
my teacher, my coach, my fan.
With love, John

And in warmest memory of a great man,
Gilberto Carrillo Robles
(1917–2001),
a second father to me.

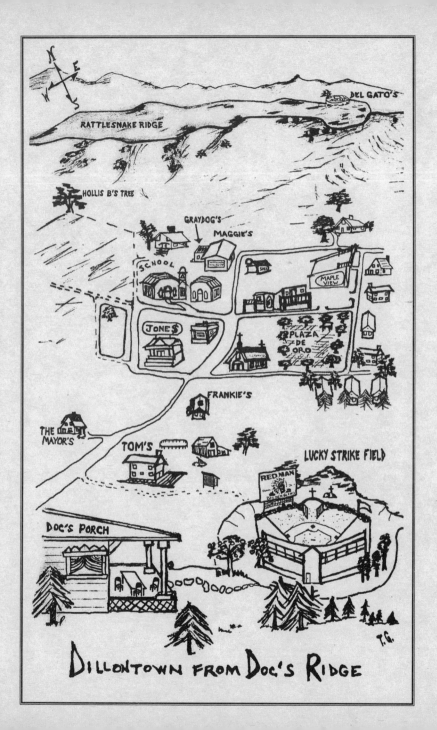

DILLONTOWN FROM DOC'S RIDGE

In the big inning . . .

People down in Dillontown don't agree on much. Not the skateboard laws. Not the billboard laws. The economy. The ecology. There's days when they don't even agree on which way the wind is blowing.

But they agree on this. From the old-timers in their overalls over on Maine Street, to the seventy-seven keyboard-clicking kids down at Scrub Oak Community School, they'll each and all tell you. If there never was a boy named Cruz de la Cruz, somebody would've come along and invented him.

And no matter how weird and wild and tall the tale, no one, not even Blackjack Buck himself, could've cooked up a mind-whacking brain-snapper as wild and woolbacious as what really happened.

Why?

Because Cruz de la Cruz, that cyber-*vato* desperado, not only saved *el civismo*, the very spirit of this town, he saved the holy game of baseball as we know it.

1

Tom Gallagher sensed the ghostly calm even before he opened his eyes. In a hill town known for its harsh and wild winds, the morning broke without even the whisper of a breeze.

Tom had hoped today would be as ordinary as possible. He'd woken early, dressed, and finished off a plate of his mother's *chorizo con huevos,* as he usually did on a Sunday morning. Then he'd walked outdoors to pay his friendly old neighbor, Doc Altenheimer, a friendly old visit, as he usually did on Sundays. He'd stopped to pick up the paper at the foot of Doc's long driveway, as usual. But today, Tom was planning to do something *un*usual.

"Hey, Doc!" he called as he hustled toward the huge white house. "Padres are in third!"

"Well, what do you know," Doc called back. "There's hope yet, isn't there?"

The eighty-seven-year-old apple rancher sat at a yellow kitchen table set smack in the middle of his long front porch. He leaned out and slid a chair over the wooden deck boards.

"Come have a seat, Tom." Doc talked like he moved, slow and easy. "Good to see a friendly face. My gosh, with that Town Hall meeting coming up tonight, everybody and their brother's been by here lately, trying to sell me on one fool plan or another."

Doc's words hit Tom two ways. First, he felt instantly guilty, since he was here to do the very same thing. Tom wanted to make sure, once and for all, that Doc understood this whole land-development scheme some people were pushing for was a bad idea.

Then he felt double nervous. Tom had spent all week working on a little speech. Never in his twelve and a half years had he done anything like that before—to write out a speech ahead of time in order to remember what to say when the time comes.

Should be easy, right? All he had to do was to step up and deliver his pitch, just the way he'd practiced it. Well, not so easy for Tom Gallagher. Even though his father was a teacher—who spoke to crowds—and his mom was the school librarian—who read to crowds—Tom was far more comfortable keeping his thoughts to himself, even with his friends.

"Yesterday," said Doc, "the mayor stopped by for about the hundredth time. Him and that new banker fellow from Texas who's been buying up all the land." Doc opened up the sports pages with soft, tremoring hands. He spread out the baseball section so Tom could read him the scores.

"Funny, ain't it, son? Now that it's all come down to me, it looks like I took over being the most popular and the least popular man in town at the same time."

Tom puffed out a small laugh. He'd heard that phrase lots of times in these hills, but never in regards to Doc. There was a shadowy former pro baseball player named Dante Del Gato, a one-time hometown hero, who officially wore that title. Nowadays, the man was practically a hermit, living on top of Rattlesnake Ridge.

"After the mayor left," Doc continued, "the Historical Society came calling. Daisy Ramirez and that bunch of busybodies. Tried to tell me that this old, broken-down baseball field was a *historical monument.* Oughta be preserved. Well, I told 'em, it's history, all right. Soon as I sell the land, it'll be history." Doc laughed. "They didn't appreciate that."

Sell the land? *Wait a minute!* Just yesterday Tom had reassured the other ballplayers, saying, "Trust me on this. Doc won't sell. He's a baseball man. And he loves these hills. He used to walk up his ridge, spot the perfect big-leaf maple tree, trim off a branch, and make his own bat from it. He's on our side."

Now Tom wondered how he could've been so wrong. "You mean, you might—you might actually—"

"I'm leaning that way, son," said Doc. "Trouble is, I've gone round and round on this deal so many times, I feel like a windmill in a windstorm. But tonight's the big night, isn't it? Got to let everyone know tonight." He took out a handkerchief, held it against his mouth, and coughed.

Now, Tom told himself. Tell him now! Don't wait another second.

Tom scooted his chair closer. He gripped the seat bottom. Then he scooted back. He closed one eye and tried to focus on his mission. Then he closed the other. He saw the words, but he could not make himself speak.

"I ain't a fool, Tom. Sure, it means more traffic and noise

and bulldozers kicking up dust all year long. But all in all, I think it'll be good for us. This place is dying, son. And as far as I can see, there's only one way to pump life and spirit back into Dillontown. Open up the highway, build new roads and new homes, and bring in more jobs. Those builders did nice enough work down the hill. I expect they'll do the same up here." He tucked away his handkerchief. "Wouldn't be selling 'em my land if I didn't. Jumpin' jackrabbits, what do I need with six million dollars, man my age?"

That nearly knocked Tom off his chair backwards. *Six million dollars?* That much? Well, Doc, he thought, you could give it to me. But Tom had never considered the idea that a man might reach a point in life when even a million dollars was not important.

And Tom had seen the new ballpark down in Lake View Mesa, the shiny chain-link fences and store-bought grass, all neat and trim. He'd seen the new baseball camp whose summer team began an annual challenge game against the Dillontown camp three years ago. Some challenge. Each year, they'd beaten Tom and the Dillontown Wildcats by at least ten runs.

Maybe brand-new and improved *was* better.

For the next half hour, Tom pored over the sports pages for Doc, their usual ritual. He'd call out each game result and the box score highlights, and each time, Doc had something wise and thoughtful to contribute.

"Don't count them Pirates out of it just yet. Those young players've got more heart and hunger than all them overpaid millionaires combined!"

Tom nodded, but in his brain all he could do was yell at himself. *Why didn't I talk to him sooner?* Why'd I keep putting it off? And why can't I tell him now that I think we're losing the greatest ballpark in the world, with a hundred years of baseball swirling its walls and a right-hand batter's box that holds the very same dirt that Dante Del Gato once dug into and spat into on his way into the world-record books?

Slowly, Tom found the next score, the Yankees game, and was about to read it out when Doc spoke up again.

"You know, I've been here all my life. My wife and son, God hold them close, lived and died right here. Even in hard times, this town's been good to me." He set his elbows on the table and laced his fingers together. "And I just hope to return the favor. That's all."

Tom sat back and stared off into the distance. From Doc's front porch, he could see the spires and crosses of several churches rising above the scattered rooftops of the town below. He could see the shops on Maine and Mercado, the little adobe post office and Town Hall, and La Plaza de Oro, where a cluster of old ladies in white scarves stood feeding the birds before making their way to Mass.

Closer, near the apple groves and farmlands, he could see the ancient baseball field—Lucky Strike Park—built on a dry lake bed a hundred years ago by Doc's father and a gang of crusty gold miners, including Mr. "Long John" Dillon himself, the founder of the town.

Doc still owned Lucky Strike Park, but more importantly, he owned a total of 320 acres of prime real estate, which was key to the whole deal. Doc's land was where the golf course would go, where the best homes would be built, and where the new lake had been planned—a lake that would drown the town's baseball field under fifteen feet of water.

Doc coughed again, wiped his mouth, while his eyes seemed fixed on empty air about halfway to the orange trees on the edge of his front lawn.

"For fifty-five years, I delivered just about every baby born in this town, Tom, including you. So I figure I can deliver the town this one last gift. A new park and a chance for a new life."

Tom's stomach wrenched tighter. He lowered his head. No sense now saying anything. Doc had made his decision and he'd made his peace with it.

Ever since the early 1900s, the Altenheimer family had leased Lucky Strike Park to the townspeople for a dollar a year. This summer, the 100-year lease was up. And over that 100 years, Dillontown had shrunk from 5,000 people down to 559, give or take. Meanwhile, to the west, an ocean of red-tiled rooftops—houses and malls—had crept along the land, coming closer and closer, like a pool of blood oozing up out of the earth itself.

"Once those builders put in a spanking-new field, Tom, it'll be a whole lot better for your team, don't you think? Better facilities. Better equipment. My gosh! Look what it did for those boys down the hill."

For some reason, hearing that fired up a spark in Tom. At the same moment, a breeze began to stir. "Those guys aren't so great," he said. "Just because they got a fancy park with batting cages and everything doesn't make them such great ballplayers. Our field's just as good. And we like it!"

The east wind gusted up and rustled the paper on the table. Tom slammed his arm down to catch it. Then he said something that surprised him as much as it seemed to startle Doc. "Shoot, we could stomp those guys like a bush on fire any day of the week."

Doc pulled back and smiled. "Well, you haven't done it yet."

Tom folded his arms. "Still, we could beat 'em. If we really wanted to. Like the Pittsburgh Pirates, like you said, we got heart. We do. And hunger. Those other games just never meant anything, that's all."

Doc sat a moment longer. "I like your spirit, Thomas. Your age, I was the same way." He took a black pen from his pocket. On the sports page margin, he began to write. Doc often left Tom with a few words to ponder, "words of encouragement," he called them. This time he wrote, *Even in the dead of night, the sun is always shining.*

He replaced the pen. "Nice to hear you speak up, though. But the plain fact is, times've changed. I'm sorry, Tom. It's just too late."

As Doc had promised, that night, in front of five hundred people sitting on five hundred rickety metal folding chairs, with another few dozen crowded around the edges of the rickety, crickety Town Hall, he let the whole world know what he'd decided to do.

Tom sat in the far back row with Frankie Flores, his best friend, alongside Ramón Sabala and a few other kids who'd signed up for the 12-and-Under Wildcat Baseball Camp. Sitting nearby were Tom's parents, along with Rachel Gleason, the quietest girl in school, and her little sister, Tara, who was not so little, but, as she put it, "big-boned." Next to them sat Frankie's loudmouthed cousin, María.

They all strained to see the color graphics the builder flashed on the video screen showing fancy ranch houses with mountain views, a golf course with slick greens and white sand traps, and a combo sports field. Next came shots of families playing soccer, golfers hitting golf balls, and little baby ducks floating on a blue lake. It was a fancy, professional show, and Tom could tell people were impressed.

Finally the lights came on. Doc stood up and walked to the podium. And it seemed like the whole room sucked in one big breath at once.

"As I've said all along," Doc began, "I only want what's best for this town. I'm sick of all the feuding and the brouhahas. Too old for all that. But I'm also too old to look after my land." While he spoke, Doc tipped back his white silk cowboy hat and took in the whole crowd with his silvery blue eyes. "These men from Orange County came down here and made me a decent offer. They'll widen the road, put in some nice homes, throw up a new park for the kids. From the get-go, it all sounded good to me."

Doc glanced at a cluster of other big landowners sitting right up front, including Ray Pruitt, a cattle rancher; Alabaster Jones, the bank president; and Mayor Oscar Calabaza. They all owned big spreads near Doc's land. They all knew that if Doc's property got developed, then the value of their land would go sky-high.

"But early this morning," Doc continued, "a fine young ballplayer came to visit me. And he had a few things to say that put a hitch in my hat."

Tom's heart thumped against his chest bones like a bad-hop grounder. He sank low into his seat.

Doc wetted his lips. "Now, I ain't much of a churchgoer, you folks know that. But here's what I do believe. Dillontown is a baseball town. And that makes whatever we do here a baseball decision. And since I also believe that baseball is God's game, then I'll put the fate of this town in His hands."

The whole crowd rumbled, swiveled. They all turned to ask their neighbors if they'd heard right. Had they heard what this old codger'd said?

Doc raised a hand. "Now, hold on. Don't jump out ahead of me. These fine gentlemen stood here and told us how beneficial their housing project has been for those families down the hill. How much more advantage and opportunity their children have than our kids do up here. And I felt the same way. But what young Tom Gallagher said today set me to wondering. Is it new facilities that would help this town the most, or a new *spirit*?" His eyes roamed the room. "So here's what I've decided to do."

Tom sank even lower. Everyone twisted and turned to look at him.

Doc's voice rose up loud and strong. "I hereby propose a good old-fashioned baseball game to settle the matter. A team from that new summer camp down the road versus a team from our camp here in town. Like they've done the past few years, only this time it's really going to mean something. One Big Game. Do or die. If our team wins, I pull out of this deal and this town stays the way it is. If they lose, bring on the bulldozers." He touched the brim of his hat. "Thank you kindly." He stepped away from the podium. No one said a word. His boot clicks filled the hall.

Tom was now crouched on the floor. María Flores, tall and lean, towered above, one hand on her hip. "You said he was on our side!" she hissed. "That you were going to talk to him for us. What'd you say?"

"I don't know!" Tom squeaked out. "I didn't say *anything*."

"I don't get it," said Rachel. "*Us?* Mr. Gallagher, does he mean *us?*"

Tom's dad, the camp coach, had a look on his face that said it all. His mouth hung open like a sand trap. His eyes were as big as golf balls.

"That's not fair!" said Tara. "We'll never win. And when we lose, everyone'll hate us and blame us for the rest of our lives."

Frankie leaned over and swatted Tom's shoulder. "I kind of like the idea," he said. "I bet every girl in town will be at that game."

Ramón shook his head. "You'd say that about a funeral, you dog."

Tom buried his head in his hands. "You guys!" he said. "It *will* be a funeral. Ours!"

And that was precisely the feeling Tom Gallagher woke up with the next morning—as if he were going to a funeral.

The stranger rode in from the east.

Under the rays of the rising sun, through the dust of a swirling wind, the horseman rode downslope, down Rattlesnake Ridge, just as Blackjack Buck had seen in a vision, dreamed in a prophecy, a century ago.

In his rifle scabbard, laced low and tight, he carried a baseball bat made of hand-cut mountain maple, custom-lathed, and sanded to a shine.

Some say he rode in on a Santa Ana wind. Some say, on the lonesome trill of an elderberry flute. But everyone in this old town, Dillontown, set high in the California wildback near the Mexican line, will always remember that day.

It was a day of disaster, following a night of disaster, following several years of discord and disaster, the day Cruz de la Cruz came to town.

Monday morning, Tom Gallagher lay in bed listening to the windy rustle of trees outside as a wave of sadness broke inside of him. He hated that feeling. Imagine feeling sad in the middle of summer vacation. Imagine feeling sad on the first day of baseball camp.

But when you knew it would be the last camp ever on a special field, when you knew that the mountains you roamed by foot and by horseback would soon be scraped off and bulldozed flat, and when you knew that it would be your own dumb fault, it was hard not to feel sad.

If only Tom had known what Doc Altenheimer was going to say last night, he would've kept his mouth shut and avoided this whole mess. But Tom also realized that keeping his mouth shut had *caused* this whole mess. *If only he'd spoken up sooner!*

Tom knew how his parents felt about the deal. Besides running the Wildcat Baseball Camp, his mom and dad both worked at Scrub Oak Community School.

"We've got empty shops up Maine Street and down Mercado," his dad had said. "We need this housing project to bring in more people and build up the town's tax base. More taxes means more money for schools and libraries."

Tom's mother wouldn't have it. "Our schools and libraries will do just fine without all those dreary look-alike houses. *And* the traffic *and* the noise. When I look out my window, Jerry, I want to see mountaintops, not rooftops. And you used to say the same thing! Besides, it's been proven that mountain views are soothing to the soul. They relax the brain."

"Well, sure. I know that. But at some point we need to think about where our money will come from. And mountains don't pay taxes."

For the most part, they'd left it at that—a hot topic that sizzled between them.

"Tom, get up!" Frankie Flores ran into the bedroom and cannonballed onto his best bud's bed. "Baseball camp, *compadre!*"

Tom wrapped the pillow around his head. "Get off. You're suffocating me."

Frankie slid down to the floor. "Oh, my girlfriends say the same thing—I leave them breathless." He bopped Tom on the thigh. "Come on, no time to snooze, we got to cruise and get everything ready, Freddie."

Slowly, Tom rolled over. The poor guy, he thought. Frankie didn't realize that the world had changed overnight, that disaster was upon them, that the field where they'd grown up playing one-on-one, make-believe ball games—the field where the San Diego Padres battled the New York Yankees for nine full innings, where the Cubs met the Cardinals or the Mariners faced the Mets on an April morn—would soon be only a memory.

"What's the use?" said Tom. "No one's going to show up now. No one wants to get slaughtered in the Big Game and have everyone blame them for turning Dillontown into Lake View Mesa *Two*."

"You think we're going to get slaughtered? With me and Wil and Josemaria and Kevin and everybody? Forget it, *'mano*! We're going to be heroes. And you are, too. I'll make sure of that." He backhanded Tom on the leg. "I mean, hey, you're my *hermano*, my bro, *mi vato*! Eh?"

Tom didn't answer. He lay perfectly flat on his back, breathing slowly, while staring at the tattered poster of Dante Del Gato, the mystery man, on his closet door.

After a moment, he shifted his gaze from Del Gato to Tony Gwynn and Sammy Sosa pinned above his computer screen. He always felt like these three baseball legends were watching him, ready to offer their wisdom. What would they say now if they thought he was giving up?

"Hey, buddy," Tony Gwynn would call out. "Get up and go! I've told you a hundred times, you're a great player."

Then Sammy Sosa would add, "Tomás, *escuche*. You got more power than I ever had when I was twelve. *Digame*, what's your secret?"

But the notorious Dante Del Gato—the guy Tom considered the most amazing player who ever lived—he would only shrug, saying, "You want to end up like me? Fine. Quit. Who's stopping you?"

Tom kept breathing, relaxing every muscle in his arms, back, shoulders—even his scalp. Today he would listen to Sosa and Gwynn.

"What's with the smile?" said Frankie. "What's so funny?"

Tom wiggled his head, then popped up off the bed. "Nothing."

Later that morning, just before nine, Tom and Frankie headed out the barn door and across the backyard. Over their shoulders, they each carried a bag of baseball gear, balanced high to compensate for the headwind.

Mr. Gallagher stepped out of the kitchen and onto the back deck, clutching his clipboard and a box of new baseballs. "Is that barn all cleaned up, gentlemen? Ready to go?"

The barn had a bunkhouse in the rear where the farmhands used to stay in the olden days. The boys in camp would be using the bathroom and showers in there.

"Clean as my grandma's kitchen," called Frankie. Then he whispered, "Don't tell him my grandma raises pigs in her kitchen."

"She *races* pigs in her kitchen?" Tom teased.

Frankie didn't miss a step. "Yeah, man. She goes hog wild."

As they approached the henhouse, Mr. Gallagher caught up and asked, "What's the final tally, Tom?"

"The final tally," Tom repeated. The words took a moment to register. He grabbed his blue notebook—his Dreamsketcher, he called it—from his hip pocket and flipped it open. "Well, we got four more cancellations this morning. That leaves maybe ten who are still coming." *Eight* was more like it. But for the time being, Tom had penciled in *Sosa* and *Gwynn*—just in case.

Mr. Gallagher sighed. Tom knew he was disappointed. Last year they had over twenty players in camp.

The trio crossed the dirt road and headed toward the baseball diamond on Doc Altenheimer's land.

Tom's notebook was his mom's idea. Since his mom was a librarian, Tom had grown up hearing her read stories out of every book in the school library, from the science of baseball to coyote tales. Then, last year, she started buying him special blank books covered in blue leather that snapped shut with black elastic bands. She said these books were for his *own* stories, and he carried one with him at all times. Since they were just the right size to slip into his pocket, Tom used them for everything from baseball stats to fantasy tales to sketches of grandmas racing pigs.

Sometimes he wrote words and sometimes he just doodled. Whenever his mind drifted off someplace interesting, he'd draw what he saw or jot a thought into his book. Then later, he'd turn the whole thing into a *dreamsketch*, as he called it. But the book was not a diary, Tom insisted. Nor was it a journal.

He wrote no silly secrets in his notebook, no gossip, no blah-blah recitation of the day's events. He found all that stuff boring. The problem with journals, Tom decided, is that they're always about "What is." Tom preferred to write about "What if?"

"What if you could saddle up a satellite and ride around the earth?" "What if your brain waves could stop the wind, then start it up again?" "What if a quiet, uncoordinated kid loved baseball with such pure passion that his passion became talent, the way a caterpillar becomes a butterfly, and turned him into a super-mega-superstar, even though he's only twelve?"

As Tom crested the rise above the baseball field, his eyes fell upon White Fang Peak, the highest point on Rattlesnake Ridge.

Just a few miles away, near the top of that peak, lived a man who once had the same kind of passion for baseball that Tom had. Lots of times during Little League games, Tom had stared at that mountain from his position in right field just thinking about the man inside. And his secrets.

The guy was unapproachable, a mumbling recluse of the worst sort, according to all reports. Still, Tom was fascinated by what he'd done.

Dante Del Gato. Even today, that name alone could scandalize and shambalize the hearts and minds of baseball fans across the land. Back in the early '80s, Del Gato was an outfielder for the San Diego Padres. He was the league's most valuable player and batting champ. Naturally, he was a home-town hero, since he was born and raised right here in Dil-lontown. He was also the only player in history ever to hit a home run clear out of old Jack Murphy Stadium. A cloud-busting blast! Some 545 feet.

But on the opening day of the '84 World Series, when the Padres were set to face the Detroit Tigers, Dante Del Gato was nowhere to be found. And he never showed up the whole week long, as the Tigers ate the Padres for dinner and won the World Series, four games to one.

He had been perfect in the play-offs. In five games against the Cubs, he went nineteen-for-nineteen at the plate. Then he walked away. And no one could ever understand why.

That is, no one except Tom. Lots of people had theories, but Tom understood. At least he thought so. You see, Tom un-derstood disappearing. He would cross the street just to avoid a couple of girls from school. He would ride into the hills for hours, just searching for ancient Indian sites or big-leaf maple trees. So to be hounded by packs of reporters and fans, to be in the public spotlight while trying to play perfect baseball—Tom could certainly imagine the pain and pressure of that. Of course, he'd never done anything as huge as letting down a ball team bound for its very first World Series.

Until now. This might do it, he figured. Putting his team in a spot where they had to beat the Lake View Vikings in order to preserve the town—along with a hundred years of baseball tradition—might one day rank right up there with saying *adiós* to a team headed for the Series.

Before he started down the embankment, Tom spotted the

dusty rooster tail of a farm truck rising off the dirt road lead- ing to the ballpark.

"Frankie," he said. "Here comes your uncle and your snobby cousin María. And there's Wil Barnes behind them."

Tom watched the vehicles approach. And soon his mood began to change. Soon, this ancient baseball field built in a puny lake bed, with its plywood-covered grandstands and peeling blue paint, its sunken-pit, stone-wall dugouts with their sway-back timber roofs, the brown tumbleweeds bunched up against the backstop—soon the whole bedrag- gled ballpark came alive with possibilities. It was almost as if the field had a spirit of its own.

In all, seven more baseball campers—four boys and three girls—had arrived, making a grand total of nine. They each crawled up onto the bleachers under the wooden roof while Mrs. Gallagher added their names to her list. Now, at least, they had a full team.

Clifford Villanova was a surprise. He'd just moved here from the Pala Indian Reservation up north to live with his grandparents. Clifford sprang up to the top row and sat next to Wil "Big as a Barn" Barnes, whose father owned the tack and feed. Below them sat Rachel and Tara Gleason. In the next row down, balancing a telescope across his knees, Ramón Sabala tapped away on his handheld computer. On the bottom plank, little Cody Pomroy, who, like Tara, was only eleven, sat next to Frankie. Right away, Frankie chal- lenged him to a sunflower-seed-spitting contest.

"See if you can hit my cousin," urged Frankie. "Use the wind."

María Flores, who was tall, strong, and could scare the breath out of any boy in town, shot up when she heard the challenge. "Try it, you little gob of troll snot, and I'll dump you in that trash can and rip off your toes." And everyone knew she could do it.

Troll snot, thought Tom. Good words. Secretly, he wrote them down.

"Frankie, Cody," said Mr. Gallagher. "Appropriate behavior, please." He looked up. "All right, listen, everyone. I need your attention."

With those words, Tom drifted off on another thought, far over the stone archway in center field. He knew his father. To him, talking became a teaching moment, and teaching became preaching, and Tom had learned long ago when to tune him out.

In a moment, he'd leaned back and settled his eyes on an elderberry bush halfway up a nearby hill. Its yellow flowers waved like banners in a stadium, sending Tom off into one of the ballparks in his mind. There he found the stands filled with a roaring crowd. The locker room was a-jumble with beard-stubbled men who sat bare-chested, suiting up for the game of a lifetime, taping broken finger bones to healthy fingers, spitting tobacco juice on blue-black bruises, singing and cussing like two dozen bravado boys trying to hide their yard-dog jitters.

In that world, Tom would talk to these men, and they would listen. He would snarl his words, and they would whoop and nod. He would laugh at their fears, and they would laugh louder.

Then he would stand and lead them to battle, waving a bat over his head. He would—

"Tom?" said his father. "Tom, are you with us?"

Tom lowered his gaze from White Fang Peak to look at his dad. "Yeah." He glanced around. "Yeah, I'm listening."

"I asked you a question. Ramón's mother, Mrs. Sabala, wondered if we could expect any more players. You said about ten or so, right?"

All eyes turned toward Tom.

With shaky hands, he opened his Dreamsketcher, counted names, counted heads, then said softly, "No, no one else. Everyone's here."

"Only nine guys?" said Wil. "We can't go into that game with only nine players! That's ridiculous. No backup, no relievers. What if someone gets hurt?"

That's not what he really meant. Tom—and everyone else—knew that Wil meant they couldn't go into the Big Game with *these* nine players. And more specifically, they were bound to lose with a starting lineup that included Tara, Cody, and Tom.

Mr. Gallagher studied the squad. "Well, I see a scrappy bunch here. But before we talk about relief pitchers, first we'll need a *starting* pitcher."

"Hey, I'll pitch," said María. "And I can't even pitch. But so what? We have to play this game and we have to win. I don't want tons of people moving up here."

Clifford jumped in. "She's right. Besides, who are these guys? A bunch of all-stars?" He grinned at everyone with big white teeth that shined against his dark skin. But Clifford had only been here since January, so he had no clue that, yes, in fact, the Vikings team was full of all-stars.

Oh, man, thought Tom, what a *disaster*. What did I get us into? This game will be pure humiliation for all of us.

Frankie stood. "I say we get more players. Come on, Tom. Let's call some guys up. What about Josemaria? And where's Kevin and Troy?"

"They all canceled this morning," Tom answered. "Their e-mails said they're going down the hill to a soccer camp."

Frankie slumped. "Traitors."

"Exactly," said María. "So forget those guys. Forget anybody who didn't have the guts to show up. Hey, we got nine. That's enough."

Then an idea hit Tom like a beanball bonking his helmet. What if *I* didn't show up? If I drop out, that'll leave just eight—not enough for a team—so then there'd be no game. Then Doc would have to make up his own mind. And this time, I'd help him. Yeah, that's perfect. *I'll quit.*

On the ball field, a dust devil kicked up, swirling around home plate. Several sun-dried candy wrappers lifted up into the sky.

Tom sat back, watching, but he could not relax. Was this really what he wanted to do? And could he do it? Could he make himself announce to everyone that he was quitting?

As he looked out toward White Fang Peak, a doubt began to rise. Dante Del Gato had quit. And look what happened to him. But what else could Tom do? This was all his fault. What else could he *possibly do*?

He clutched his Dreamsketcher to his ribs to keep from

shaking. He closed his eyes. He took a breath. He felt the wind blow stronger. But before he could sputter a sound, Tara stood up and pointed into the distance. "Hey, look at that!"

All heads turned.

Cresting over the dirt bank beyond center field came a horse and rider. Everyone watched as the horseman slowly made his way down the steep bank and through the iron gates beneath the stone archway.

"Do you believe this?" said Frankie.

"Not yet," said Wil.

Straight through center field he rode. Stretched across the back of his speckled white horse was a duffel bag and bedroll. The rider, Tom could now see, was a boy, about twelve, wearing a scruffy cowboy hat, blue jeans, black boots, and a pearl-buttoned shirt.

He rode right up to home plate.

Burned into the skirt of his saddle in fancy black letters were the words *Cruz-on.com*. Full saddlebags hung down on both sides. Next to his knee, in a leather rifle scabbard, he carried a wooden baseball bat.

The boy dismounted and led his horse through the side gate near the dugout and under the grandstand canopy, where the players sat with eyes like frogs, alert, agog.

The stranger removed his crumpled Stetson. "Morning," he said. *"Buenos días."* He looked at everyone with a shy grin. "Is this the world-famous Dillontown Wildcats Baseball Camp?"

3

Mr. Gallagher stepped forward. "Yes, yes, it is. This is Lucky Strike Park. Home of the Wildcats." He stretched out his hand. "Welcome."

"Thank you." The boy shook, replacing his hat, then he unsnapped his shirt pocket and pulled out a piece of paper and a wad of money.

"I'm Cruz de la Cruz," he said. "From Paloma. Here's my insurance waiver and two hundred dollars. I bat right, throw right, I'm mainly a shortstop, but I can pitch or play anywhere. Hope I can still sign up."

María leaned forward. "You rode that horse all the way from Paloma? Over the mountains?"

The boy gave his sturdy horse a few sharp pats. Its silver-gray mane stood out against a white coat dotted with several brown spots the size of baseballs. He nodded, laughing. "Yeah." Then he shrugged. "Beats walking."

"That's, like, fifty miles of rough country," said Frankie. "How long'd it take?"

"Not that long. Left yesterday morning. Stopped at my uncle's house in Campo at noon, then rode to *mi abuela*'s in Pine Valley. That's where I came from this morning."

"Wow, even Pine Valley's a long ride!"

"Certainly is," said Mrs. Gallagher. "Cruz, you must be hungry."

"Oh, no, s'okay." He waved a hand. "But Screwball here, he could sure use some water."

"Of course," said Mrs. Gallagher. "We live right next door. And I'll fix you a sandwich. How's peanut butter and jelly?"

"Well, yeah, all right. Sounds good. Thank you." He bent down and dusted tiny leaves of sagebrush off his pant legs. "I'm just glad to finally be here."

Wil glanced around at the others, smiling. "You're *glad* to be here? What for?"

Cruz flashed a smile. "Seriously?" He turned and held his hand out toward the ball field. "Look at this place. The old stone wall, the gate, the famous Shrine of the Dillontown Nine. Getting to play here is like dying and going to Fenway."

"Going to where?" said Cody.

"It's in Boston, *'mano,*" hissed Frankie. "It's a ballpark."

Everyone looked out past Cruz's arm at the tired dirt field, now full of weed clumps and gopher humps since the end of Little League last month. They studied the faded-out "Red Man Tobacco" scoreboard; the slant-angle iron gates, frozen open and rusting in deep center; the dry erosion rivulets running through the outfield; the ancient stone wall, full of holes crammed with soda cans and trash. And that circular stone monument, topped with a white cross, out beyond the walls, built nearly ninety years ago as a memorial to a team of gold miners who'd died when their mine shaft collapsed. Seeing the field with an outsider's eyes, Tom felt embarrassed.

"Yes, well," said Mr. Gallagher, "it does have a certain—a certain—" He stumbled for the word.

"Spirit," said Rachel. "I think there's a sort of *spiritness* out there."

Rachel may have been quiet, but when she did speak, she usually said something profound.

Cruz's hat bobbed up and down. "Yeah," he said. "Yeah, that's right." He smiled at Rachel.

"Okay," said Ramón. "But do you know what you're walking into?"

Cruz raised his eyebrows. "Well, the website said it was a weeklong camp for anyone who loves to eat, drink, and sleep baseball. That's me!"

The website was Tom's doing, and he tended to hype it up a bit.

"That was before last night," said Wil. "Now it's eat, sleep, and *delete* baseball."

"Not necessarily," said Mr. Gallagher. "We've had a little disagreement in our town over what direction it should go in. And this ball team here will have a say in that decision."

"A *big* say," Frankie added with a grin. He was the only one smiling.

Tom's dad folded his arms against his clipboard and went on to explain the whole situation. At the end of the story, Cruz took off his hat, rubbed his hand over his long black hair, and said, "Whew. We're playing for the future of this ballpark?" He brought his hand down and made a fist. "*Ay, Dios.* Then we're on a mission from God."

At that moment, Tom's whole world shifted. Just a notch. But suddenly he realized he was looking at more than just some kooky outsider who smelled like horse and sage. He saw more than the tenth ballplayer. Tom saw a boy who could stand up to a challenge, look it in the eye, and not blink. He saw a boy who was not afraid to show how much he loved baseball, how much he loved this old ballpark and was willing to fight for it.

"Okay, then." Tom's dad clapped his hands. It was almost as if Cruz had inspired him, too. "We've got ourselves a team. Let's go set up camp."

"Cruz," said Mrs. Gallagher, "you can put your horse up in our barn across the road. We're going that way, too."

As the players grabbed their bags and bounced off the bleachers, Mr. Gallagher took Tom's arm. "You know, Tom," he started, "we all have dreams. And I don't want to limit your imagination. But you have to pay attention when you're out here. You're a part of this team. And I know I've told you this before, but unless we can all join you in your dream, then, I'm sorry, but you'll have to join us in ours. And right now, our dream is to build a team here that can win a pretty important game."

"Mine, too, Dad. Really, that's my dream, too. I'm serious."

"Then try to stay with us out here, all right?" He smiled.

Tom felt such relief, now that the new kid had shown up, that he nodded eagerly. "Don't worry. I will."

For the next two hours the Gallagher backyard was like an ant hill near a sugar spill. Players scurried in all directions. Mr. Gallagher believed that a baseball camp should be a *camp.* In all ways. So the boys pitched their tent over near the barn, and the girls put up theirs off the rear deck.

Tom's mom supervised the installation of cots, lanterns, and picnic tables. She helped the campers pick their tent leader and draw up a list of chores and rules that each camper signed. For dressing and bathing, the boys had the bunkhouse, and the girls had the downstairs guest room.

Mr. Gallagher directed a group of players to chop up eucalyptus branches and dig a campfire pit in the middle of the backyard. Afterwards, they lined the pit with stones, then set up benches all around.

Finally, everything was ready to go. Cruz stood at the woodpile, sweat pouring down his face. "Man, this is great. This is way better than I thought it would be." He yanked off his batting gloves and leaned his ax against an old tree stump. "Dillontown, I'm ready to play some ball."

"Yeah, right," said Clifford as he knelt down and collapsed onto the grass. "You go to the field and start warming up. We'll be right there."

The other players sprawled out, too, on the lawn or up against the pepper tree, drenching their heads with streams from their water bottles.

The kitchen door burst open and out came Tom's dad pulling a little red wagon stacked high with hamburger patties, buns, and all the fixings. Mrs. Gallagher was already on the deck, firing up the brick barbecue.

"Ten minutes till lunchtime," she called.

"Food!" said Wil. "Cruz, you better stick around."

"Okay, okay, I'm not going anywhere," he said, smiling. "Except maybe to the barn, to check on Screwball."

"I'll go with you!" Cody bounced up and started running.

Tom decided to join them. One by one, so did the others.

Entering the barn, Ramón put his hand on Cruz's shoulder. "So, how'd you find out about this camp, anyway?"

"Pretty easy. I was searching the Web and I saw the site."

"You were searching for baseball camps?"

"No, actually, I was searching for Dillontown."

At the sound of Cruz's voice, Screwball thrust his nose between the bars of the last stall door. "Hey, boy," said Cruz. "There you are. How you doin'? Getting enough to eat?"

"Why do you call him Screwball?" asked Tara.

"Because he's goofy." Cruz opened the stall and stepped inside. "Like me."

"What do you mean, goofy?" Tara persisted.

Cruz held Screwball's head, rubbing his whiskery nose. "Well, he does the weirdest things sometimes. One night, I come home, and he's in my room watching TV. Which I don't mind, but he should at least ask me before he tries to change the channel. I mean, did you ever see what a remote control looks like after a horse uses it?"

"Oh, that never happened," said Tara. She turned to her sister. "Don't believe him."

Rachel smiled.

Cruz looked over his shoulder. "Tom, I wanna take him outside to the corral with your horse. Be okay?"

"Yeah, I guess. Let's see how they get along."

Cruz grabbed a rope halter and slipped it over the horse's head. He turned to his saddle draped over an oil barrel in the corner, opened one of the saddlebags, and reached in.

"Here," he said to Tara. "Here's my card."

Everyone huddled close to see it:

www.Cruz-on.com
Have Fun, Will Travel
Contacto Cruzado: CCRider@Cruz-on.com

"What does that mean?" asked María. " 'Have Fun, Will Travel'?"

"That's the name of our family business. Back home, I lead trail rides into the mountains or down into the desert. My mom and I took it over after my dad died. And 'Cruz-on.com,' that's our website *and* my motto. I like seeing new places. So I'm always cruising on." He grinned at her.

"You mean, you go on pack trips," asked Tom, "and get paid for it?"

"It's crazy, I tell you. People come from all over to ride off into the hills. And they need a guide. So I lead 'em, and we just cruise on." He passed the rope to Tara. "Here, help me take him outside, okay?"

Cody ran ahead to drag open the gate. Tara followed.

As Cruz left the barn, María circled around him, facing him toe-to-toe and walking backwards. "Okay, now, tell me for real," she said. "Who are you, and why did you really come?"

"What do you mean? I just told you." Another grin and a glance at everyone. "Really, I'm not anybody special. Just a guy who wants to take Major League Baseball by storm one day."

"So you came *here*?" said Wil. "Not a bright choice, Sunshine."

"You kidding? To me, it's the perfect choice. See, there's somebody in this town who has a huge secret. The most important secret in baseball. And I want to sit down with that guy and ask him about it."

"What guy? Who?"

Cruz shrugged and answered as easy as giving out the time of day. "Dante Del Gato."

4

María froze, forcing Cruz to stop. "You mean the crazy man?"

Cruz side-shuffled and danced past her. "I mean the greatest hitter of the last fifty years. I mean the guy who holds records for the most home runs in one month, the most stolen bases by an outfielder, and the most consecutive base hits ever. The guy who went nineteen for nineteen in his last nineteen at-bats before he walked away in a cloud of mystery."

"No, no, you got it wrong," said Wil, who used his bulk and his height to shoulder up against Cruz. "You mean the guy who walked away from the World Series and left baseball in a cloud of disgrace."

Cruz shrugged and kept going. The others clustered around him like so many moons. "Well, maybe," he said. "Who really knows? That's the thing. Could've been lots of reasons for what he did."

Wil bent forward, shaking his jowls. "You got that wrong, too. My dad knows. Everyone who saw him come back to town knows. He got so hyped up and burned out on drugs or something, that he just gave up."

"Besides," said María, who elbowed closer, "you can't go see him. He lives in a fortress and he's got guard dogs all around the place."

"And electric fences!" said Cody, opening the gate for everyone. "One kid went up there and got too close and got electrocuted! Fried his skin right off. Then the dogs ate him up before anyone could find the body."

Tom listened, but could not say a word. Cruz had thought the unthinkable, spoken the unspeakable. In a strange way, the idea fascinated Tom, but at the same time, it made his stomach feel like a rodeo ring with broncos bucking left and right. Imagine someone visiting Del Gato!

Tara dropped the lead rope and narrowed her eyes. "People say Del Gato only comes out at night and runs with a pack of bloodthirsty mountain lions. That's why no one ever sees him."

Cruz nodded. "I know, I know." He rubbed Screwball about the neck and withers. "I mean, I know there's all kinds of stories about the guy. But nineteen straight hits in nineteen straight at-bats! Only two or three guys have ever done *half* that good. And he lives just a few miles away, right?"

"A few miles *uphill*. On White Fang Peak."

Cruz squinted into the east. "Well, it sounds to me like he could use a visitor"—Cruz caught Tom's eye—"or two."

After the break, everyone gathered at the baseball diamond.

"Before we get started today," said Mr. Gallagher, "I want each of you to grab a rake or a shovel or a wheelbarrow, and let's get this field into playable condition. We'll need to remove all the weeds and rocks and level out those gopher mounds."

María slumped against Rachel. "I can't believe I'm paying money for the honor of scraping weeds off a dried-out baseball field."

"But it has to look good," said Tom. "A great field for a great team." The words surprised him. Two hours ago, he never would've said something like that. But in two hours' time, a lot had changed.

For the next couple of hours the campers pulled and raked up weeds, dug out half-buried rocks, then smoothed over the rough edges of their work. Section by section, they cleared the field.

Ramón and Frankie put together a makeshift drag using old pieces of carpet wired together and weighed down with rocks and bricks. María found a length of rope and harnessed both boys to the drag like donkeys to a cart. Once a section had been cleared, they dragged the carpet back and forth over it to smooth out the dirt.

Clifford and Cruz worked on the weeds and rock piles, loading up wheelbarrow load after load, rolling them out the iron gate, and dumping them beyond the wall.

Every once in a while, María would stand up straight and survey the progress. She'd set her jaw. Then she'd force her top lip over her teeth, curl up her tongue, and whistle. Loud as a hawk screech. Made Tom jump, but Cruz would just look up from wherever he was, and María would wave him over to one pile or another, like a third-base coach signaling a charging runner to head for the plate.

By midafternoon, the field was ready for play.

As a final touch, Rachel and Cody had opened up the water hoses on it, and the dusty dirt turned a rich brown. The infield glistened in the light.

And even though the players were dead tired, they all stepped down into the sunken dugout, with its cool stone walls and pine log roof, and changed into their cleats. Some picked a partner and began playing catch. Others walked off by themselves to swing a bat.

As Tom and Frankie threw the ball back and forth, Cruz stood nearby, facing the outfield and swinging his light brown wooden bat.

"Is that a maple bat?" asked Frankie.

Cruz swiveled toward him. "Yeah."

"You like it?"

"Yeah, it's great. I made it myself."

"You did?" Frankie stopped throwing, and he and Tom walked over to inspect it. "Wow, that looks cool."

Cruz pointed to the bat barrel. "See that grain? Closer than ashwood. And maple's lighter. I think it gives the bat a springier sweet spot."

Tom knew about maple bats. Doc had made him one a couple of years ago, but it felt too small for him now. "Can I swing it?"

"Sure." Cruz passed him the smooth, warm bat. But after only one swing, Mr. Gallagher yelled, "Okay, everybody. Over here!" He stood by a group of batting stations around home plate. "Time left for one good drill."

"No such thing as a good drill," said María.

"I think you'll like this. It's on the science of hitting. Especially the science of home-run hitting."

Frankie slipped the bat from Tom's hands. "Now that's the kind of science I like." He stepped away and swung a few times as they walked.

Mrs. Gallagher read off names, and everyone was paired up with a partner. Five batting tees, which looked like black rubber ice-cream cones with a baseball on top, stood in front of the backstop.

María was still not impressed. "I thought we were going to have batting *practice*," she said. "What're the tees for?"

"That's where we'll start," said Mr. Gallagher. "First, I want to demonstrate the scientific principle behind smacking a baseball as far as you can. It's a simple matter of physics."

"Physics?" Suddenly Ramón perked up.

"No, no," said Wil. "You mean *physiques*." He flexed his arm muscles and looked around, all puffy-faced.

"No, I don't," said Mr. Gallagher. "I mean the interaction between matter"—he held up the ball—"and energy." He held up the bat. "As a hitter, you have to transfer as much energy as possible from your bat to the ball. How far the ball flies depends on how heavy your bat is and how fast you swing."

Now it was Frankie who was not impressed. "We, um, kind of already know that, Mr. G."

"Yeah," said Wil. "That's why I use the biggest bat I can find."

Mr. Gallagher held a finger aloft. "Ah, but, you see, that's a mistake. What you want, Wil, is to use the *fastest* bat you can find. It's been proven that increasing your bat speed is more important than using a heavier bat. Anybody know why?"

Oh, Dad, no! Tom thought. Frankie was joking. This isn't really a science class. Tom could see that no one even wanted to make a guess.

Finally Cruz raised his hand. "Well, I don't know. Seems to me that a big, heavy bat would just slow down your swing so that the ball would sort of plop off it and not go very far."

Mr. Gallagher snapped his fingers. "Yes, exactly."

"Wait, I don't get it." Frankie rubbed his neck. "What if you already have a fast swing and then you get a heavier bat? Even if your swing slows down a little, I think the ball would still go farther with the heavier bat."

"That's what a lot of hitters think. Big mistake. And there's scientific research to prove what I'm saying. Does anyone know why?"

"I do," said Ramón. "I know why."

"Oh, you would," said María. "Okay, *el profesor,* let's hear it."

Ramón shrugged. "It's easy. When you hit the ball, you transfer energy to it, right? The amount of energy you transfer is equal to the weight of the bat multiplied by the speed of the bat squared, all divided by two."

"Oh, right!" shouted Wil with a loud hoot. The others laughed, too, knocked shoulders, and shuffled around.

"Talk English," said Clifford.

"Talk Spanish!" said Frankie.

Ramón looked irritated. "No, really, you guys, it's true. It's a simple formula, like Einstein's. You know, E equals MC squared? Only in this case it's the *bat speed* that gets squared—not the speed of light—but in both cases, the speed has more value than the weight of the bat. That's why bat speed is more important."

"You got to be kidding." Wil swung an imaginary bat as his lips blasted apart with air. "*Einstein?* What team did *he* play for? Come on."

Ramón only shrugged again. "Take it or leave it, but the formula for why a nuclear bomb explodes is directly related to the formula for how far you can blast a baseball with a bat. It's just that in this formula we substitute the velocity of the bat for the speed of light."

"That's what I've been trying to tell you," said Mr. Gallagher. "It's physics!"

"Whoa," said María. "This is getting serious."

"Yo, Einstein," said Frankie. "You mean you could use this 'bat speed squared' thing to teach us how to hit home runs?"

"Now you're talking," said Cody.

Ramón grinned. "You wish. Look, Mr. G already told you the secret. Speed up your bat. I only told you the reason why."

"Precisely." Mr. Gallagher snapped up a ball and shook it. "And now we're going to begin a drill that's aimed at doing just that. Mrs. Gallagher has set up three stacks of bats against the backstop, from lightweight to heavy. She's also set out a pile of batting weights. I want each group to take one weight and one bat from each pile."

As his father spoke, Tom had a strange sensation. He thought he could hear the faint sounds of drumming from somewhere over the hilltop.

"Every batting station," said Mr. Gallagher, "has ten soft-skin practice balls. Each hitter will take ten swings working down from the heaviest bat to lighter to lightest. Then you'll trade places. Any questions?"

Tom looked up. Other players began to notice, too, and turned to listen. In the silence, the drumming came louder and louder.

Boom-lay, boom-lay, boom-boom-boom. Boom-lay, boom-lay, boom, ba-boom.

"What *is* that?" asked Cody.

The sound grew louder.

Within moments, the team saw heads bobbing up over the rise. Three, six, then nine. Fifteen heads in all.

Daisy Ramirez led the way, hitting two sticks together. Her son Refugio, a tenth-grader, banged a snare drum clipped to his belt. Jimbo Jakes, the apple-cider maker, beat the stretched skin of a tom-tom with two soft mallets.

Boom-lay, boom-lay, boom-boom-boom. Boom-lay, boom-lay, boom, ba-boom.

Behind the drummers came the only lawyer in town, Grayson "Graydog" LaRue, who ran a part-time law practice in back of his wife's hair salon, but mostly hung out on a bench in the plaza. He played a piccolo, blowing out a shrill, birdlike sound. With a gray goatee and a full head of wavy hair bobbing up and down, he looked like a jazzman who'd sipped a few too many espressos.

Behind Graydog marched a ragtag bunch click-clacking broken broomsticks and jangling tambourines. Frankie's mom carried a red cooler, and Maggie LaRue, Graydog's wife, carried a big stack of tortillas wrapped in paper. Others held shopping bags filled with whatever.

Off to the side, pacing back and forth, was Hollis B, the town's "poet savant," who lived on two wooden planks in a black oak tree just outside of town. Speaking into his cell phone, loudly, rapidly, Hollis B looked like a roving sideline reporter, darting around, giving reports of the band's play-by-play action to an invisible audience.

The cell phone wasn't exactly real. You see, Hollis B had a habit of walking through town, waving his arms, holding lively conversations with imaginary people. In the past, he'd scared everyone from little kids at the preschool to the group of lady bird-feeders who sat around the park.

So one day Sheriff Decker gave him an old, broken cell phone. That way, he could hold the phone up and walk around town talking like crazy and be no more annoying than a real estate agent.

Tom loved listening to him and wished that he could hear his "news report" over the clash and clang of the band.

As the group reached the ballpark fence near the dugout, Daisy Ramirez held both hands high. "Halt!"

In two steps—or in some cases, three—the band and the music came to a stop.

She turned to the campers and called out, "Wildcats! On behalf of the citizens of Dillontown, we salute you. Not only are you our baseball team, but you represent the history and spirit of this town. And now, you are the town's only hope to retain its heritage."

That last remark caused the musicians to break into a mad, electric frenzy of toots, hoots, clacks, and booms.

When they stopped, Daisy continued. "As your loyal fans, we are here to offer our support in order to help you prevail in the Big Game, the most crucial game of our lives."

"Ah, geez," said Frankie. "This is embarrassing."

Mr. Gallagher stood speechless.

Mrs. Gallagher stepped forward. "Goodness," she said. "This is—this is very nice. We thank you." She glanced at her husband. "We don't know quite what to say."

"You don't have to say anything," said Maggie, who was a great supporter of the town. She owned the In Your Face Beauty Salon, where a sign in the window read, *We'll Chop Your Mop 'Til You Say Stop.*

Today, her short brown hair was frosted blue and sprinkled with glitter. "You've got more to do than talk to us. We're just here to cheer you on. So please continue while we set up the barbecue grills, lay out the *carne asada,* some rice and beans"—she tapped the red cooler—"and Humberto's fresh salsa. We want to make sure this team is encouraged, well nourished, and plays with a flourish!"

Shrieks, whistles, and *boom-boom-boom*s filled the air again. But this time all of the ballplayers joined in.

"Carne asada!" said Frankie. "Now you're talking my lingo."

"Yo," said Wil. "If we're gonna die, why not party hearty and die happy!" María just curled her tongue and whistled five times.

While a few men helped Humberto unload the split-oil-drum grills from the back of his truck, practice resumed, and the soft-skin balls began exploding against the backstop with increasing force, particularly as the team worked its way down to the lightest stack of bats.

But after forty-five minutes or so, the sweet, smoky smell of marinated steak strips grilling over hot coals became too distracting.

"I gotta eat!" said Wil, leaning on his bat and staring toward the pile of meat.

Frankie tore off his batting gloves. "After me, *'mano.*" He started off. "Mr. G, we need a break."

Mr. G was already eating.

Soon the bleachers were filled with hungry ballplayers and their band of fans chomping down on burritos, hot from the grill, and refried beans, hot from the pan.

In a few minutes, though, everyone found out that Daisy Ramirez had more on her plate than grilled steak.

She approached Tom's dad and sat down sideways on the bleacher board, facing him. "Jerry," she said, "I'll say it straight-out. We're not comfortable with you coaching this team."

Mr. Gallagher chewed slowly and swallowed. He wiped his mouth. "Excuse me?"

Tom set down his paper plate. Fear gripped his insides. He knew what she meant. Everyone did.

Mrs. Ramirez let out a sharp breath. "Well, Jerry—no offense—but we all know what's happened in these Big Games over the last few years. Now, you're a great science teacher, don't get me wrong. But I just don't think you have the knowledge or the capability to coach these ballplayers to the point where they'd have even half a chance to win that game."

All the burrito chomping stopped. Paper plates plopped. Everyone looked at Mr. Gallagher.

Tom was amazed that his father didn't back away from the dagger-eyed glare Mrs. Ramirez aimed his way. Instead, he leaned closer.

"Well, Daisy, I understand why you might say that. But I intend to coach these kids to the best of my abilities. Yes, my baseball skills are limited, but I've downloaded a lot of excellent drills from professional coaches across the country, and I think I've put together a good program."

After he spoke, the onlookers lowered their eyes. A few grumbled.

Mr. Gallagher looked around. "Well, tell me." His voice rose. "Anyone. If you think I'm not able to run this team, let me know why."

Now Maggie spoke up. "Oh, Jerry, we all like you and think you're a great guy. But you need to understand. Last week, we figured this town had been sold down the river and its days were numbered. Then crazy ol' Doc surprised us all with this last-minute curveball he threw our way. We just want our team to have a fighting chance."

"Fighting chance, my asthma!" said Graydog. "We want them to win!" He raised his wild-weed eyebrows. "And Jerry, you're our friend, but you've been for the development. Everyone knows that. And we just don't want to be double-crossed."

Daisy Ramirez cut back in. "What Maggie and Graydog are trying to say is that these are the days of doom, like in the prophecy. And as the town historian, I need to make sure we pay heed to the warning."

"*Prophecy?*" Mr. Gallagher flicked the back of his hand her way. "That bunch of garbage? Come on, you can't be serious."

She kept talking. "We all know that as of now your intentions are to help. But over the years, the prophecies of Blackjack Buck have been shown to be historically accurate. And since the Death and Doom prophecy mentions a double-cross at the last minute—well, we can't take the chance."

"Oh, that's absurd," said Mr. Gallagher. "Look, I'm in favor of saving this town. To put it mildly, our economy stinks. We're nearly bankrupt. And we need more than one or two new shops. We need something big. A golf course is big. Construction is big. Bringing in more tax revenue, that's big. But this is all beside the point. Right now my focus is on winning this game. And why shouldn't it be? Chances are, if this deal falls through, there'll be another one right behind it."

Suddenly everyone was talking at once. It turned out that whether or not they thought Tom's dad was the double-crosser mentioned in the Death and Doom prophecy, almost no one thought he would or could give the Wildcats a "snowball's chance in *El* Centro," as Graydog put it.

Not even Tom, he had to admit.

"If we want to win," said Jimbo Jakes as he passed around cups of apple cider, "I say we get the El Cap High School coach up here. Or maybe Coach Gwynn from State."

That comment caused another storm of jawing and finger-jabbing.

"Have we got time for that?"

"I could make a few phone calls."

"But they won't work for free. Who has the money?"

Finally, Mr. Gallagher stood. "Look, if any of you have the kind of baseball knowledge you're talking about, or if you want to go out and round up someone who does, feel free.

But until you do, I'm in charge here. And as far as my commitment to this team, I intend to make sure they're well coached and well prepared, and that we play to *win*."

He walked down the bleacher boards and onto the ground. As he strode, he shouted, "Wildcats! Meet me on the field in two minutes."

No one had much to say after that. Except Hollis B. He dashed behind the bleachers, bent over, and spoke into his phone. "The fix is in, says Daisy and them. Says, Gallagher's gang ain't got the stuff, ain't up to snuff, gonna get bulldozed over like fresh cream puffs."

Cruz's eyes opened wide. He elbowed Tom. "*Who* is that guy?"

Tom shushed him with a finger to his lips as he and the others watched through the bleacher boards.

Hollis B kept dancing. "But Gallagher says he's got the chops, says he'll pull out all the stops. His team'll be ready to take the crown. And I say, boys, lay your money down. On Dillontown. I gotta go!" With a whip and a snap, he shut the phone and high-stepped it out of there, over the boundary berm.

"Whoa!" Cruz looked around and grinned. "That's what I call talking! That's talking like he was *born* talking! Who is he?"

"That's Hollis B," said Ramón. "He lives in a tree."

"Yeah, but he's out of it, most of the time," added Rachel.

Cruz was still smiling. "Well, I like his style. And his prediction. Really, you guys. I don't see why we can't beat any team we face." The others were too polite to respond, but they shared knowing looks, then began moving down toward Mr. Gallagher, waiting on the field below. Cruz, however, casually resumed munching on his burrito.

Tom gathered some trash around him, crunched up his paper plate, and prepared to leave as well. But before he could rise, Cruz leaned over and whispered, "You know where Dante Del Gato lives, right?"

Tom nodded.

Cruz pointed with his burrito, off toward Rattlesnake Ridge. "Think you could take me there? In the dark?"

That night, after a full-blown carne asada fiesta, ten sore, gruff, and overstuffed campers crawled onto ten army surplus sleeping bags covering ten army surplus beds. No campfire, no campfire songs. *Nada.*

Mr. and Mrs. Gallagher placed their own sleeping bags under the fiberglass cover on the back deck, not far from the girls' tent, where they could keep an eye on everyone.

Inside the boys' tent, the air was heavy with the odor of sweaty shoes, socks, and forty years of dust and must. Wil huffed and puffed, creaking against his cot. "Why's it so crowded in here? I thought this was supposed to be a ten-man tent."

"That's without these cots," said Frankie. "Besides, you take up enough room for two or three guys alone."

"Now I know how a sardine feels," said Clifford.

"Now you know how a sardine smells," said Frankie.

Cruz burst in through the tent flaps. "Hey, you guys. What do you think about sleeping under the stars tonight? It's so stuffy in here."

Ramón was first to answer. "I was thinking the same thing. Besides, I want to watch the moonrise through my telescope."

Wil jumped right up. "Ramón, you rule."

Within minutes, all seven boys had grabbed their bags and dragged them outside. In the center of the lawn, just beyond a gnarly, umbrella-branched pepper tree, they threw their pillows into a small circle, then laid their bags out from there like spokes on a wheel.

It'd been almost a year since Tom had slept outside, but he remembered right away what he liked most about it. The sky. The mountain sky was filled with thousands of stars, from tiny, dim ones to some as bright as airplane lights. And they went all the way down. That's what he liked the most. In every inch of sky, from the middle of the diamond dome all the way down to the hills and trees, stars pinpricked the night.

"You know," said Cruz, "I could lie here and look at stars all night."

"Yeah, me, too," said Tom.

"I could look at 'em all day," said Frankie. "Except that, the problem with daytime is, if you see one star, you've seen 'em all."

"Frankie," said Clifford. "Put a jalapeño in it. We're trying to sleep."

The group fell silent, as if the stars demanded their full attention. Though the night was warm, Tom climbed inside his bag and brought it up to his chin. Nearby, Ramón stepped about, setting up his tripod and telescope. In the distance, some fifty yards away, Tom could hear the muffled sounds of his father on the back porch, snoring.

Once they'd all shifted into position, and Ramón turned off the lantern, Tom asked Cruz a question he'd been saving all day long.

"What was it like?" he said. "Riding all this way, all by yourself?" It was hard for Tom to imagine being so free.

Cruz tucked his hands behind his head. "It was the greatest thing I've ever done."

"Really?"

"No doubt."

"Like what?" asked Cody. "What do you mean?"

"Well, I don't know. I've been on a bunch of horseback trips, but you're always out there with other people. It's different when you're all alone."

"Your mom let you do it?" asked Frankie. "She didn't care?"

"My mom—she's not like a typical mother. She made a trip like this once when she was about my age. And she knows me. She knew I'd be okay. I called her this morning before I left my grandma's house to check in. And I called her tonight. That's all she wants."

"Wow, that is so cool," said Frankie. "I'd like to have a mom like that."

"Who wouldn't?" said Cody. "She must really trust you."

Cruz rolled over onto his stomach. "Well, yeah, but it's more than that. She knows about traveling. That traveling is like—it's like a jolt to your body. When you hit the trail, everything is brand-new, nothing's the same as at home. And when you're out there all alone, it's even better. You go when you want, you stop when you want. Your eyes see everything. Like a roadrunner zipping across a field. Or a blue-bellied lizard doing push-ups on a warm rock. You hear stuff you usually never notice." He paused a moment. "Like the cracklesnap of a cottontail running over twigs. You smell all the brush, the pine trees, your horse, the leather. It's like—I don't know— it's like you're hyper alive."

Hyper alive! Tom loved that. And *cracklesnap*. What a word! No wonder Cruz had laughed so much listening to Hollis B today. Cruz was a born talker, too.

And Tom knew exactly what Cruz was talking about. Every time he walked the hills, jumping rocks, cutting through the brush, Tom would feel a "jolt to his body." Hyper alive, hyper alert, his eyes peeled for snakes or bones or anything wild. Bursting out of a thick stand of sagebrush and stumbling upon a rainwater creek, or spotting an ancient Kumeyaay camp in the bright morning sun, would set him dream-sketching for hours. He'd run his hand over a warm bedrock boulder, feel the grinding hole, worn smooth by centuries of other hands pushing against it with round river rocks, crushing ripe acorns into meal.

Tom wanted in the most desperate way to reach under his pillow and grab his Dreamsketcher to write down some of those words and draw the scenes. But for Tom, writing was a lot like walking in the mountains. Or like Cruz's horseback trip into Dillontown. It's something he felt best doing all alone, with no one watching.

Cruz sat up and swung his legs around. "Now I got a question for you guys," he said. "What's this prophecy thing everybody's talking about?"

No one spoke. The question hit Tom like a fastball to the gut. He knew the story best and felt everyone silently urging him to answer. But he couldn't. He did not want Cruz to know.

Finally, as the silence grew too intense, Frankie reacted. "Ah, it's nothing. This town's full of dumb stories and legends."

Leave it to Frankie, thought Tom, to downplay something that might make Cruz feel uncomfortable.

"True ones," said Cody. "They're all true."

"No, they're not," Frankie countered. "The only true ones are about certain beautiful girls and me."

"Yeah, right," said Ramón, looking up from the eyepiece. "Let me see. Yes, I think one was called The Legend of the Girl Who Kissed a Boy and Puked for Days."

The bags rumbled with pounding fists and muted howls.

When things resettled, Ramón, *el profesor,* left his telescope and sat back down. "Okay, look, here's all it is," he said. "A long time ago, there was this prospector named Blackjack Buck who came here from Yuma, Arizona. He was part Quechan Indian, part Irish, and part ghost-talker. I mean, that's what people say. But he did have this talent for seeing the future. And that's pretty much it."

"That's it?" said Cruz. "That's huge! What was he, like a psychic?"

"I don't know, but every time he got just enough gold dust, he'd head into town and straight for the wine barrel room behind St. Anthony's. He'd trade for a cask of black-elderberry-and-applejack wine. Blackjack, they called it. And after he drank a bunch and shot up the town a little, he'd wander back to the church to sleep it off. But sometimes, he woke up with a vision, or a prophecy, and they always seemed to come true."

"Not always," said Frankie. "People only remember ones that did."

"He predicted the big drought of 1912 to 1916," said Wil. "And he predicted the huge flood that ended it."

"Lucky guess. He didn't even say when. He just said it would happen. Shoot, wait long enough and anything can happen."

Wil was not to be denied. "What about the collapse of the Number Nine Mine? He saw that coming."

"Yeah," said Cody. "He predicted John Dillon's death *and* his own."

"All nine miners," Wil explained to Cruz, "who just happened to be the town's baseball team, died in that one. That's why there's that stone monument out past center field."

"Another lucky guess," said Frankie. "He said, 'A team of nine will meet their fate.' I mean, go search these hills and you'll find *ninety* miners who got buried up there. Anybody could've predicted that."

Cody had more. "Maybe, but 'Crashes to crashes, dust to dust, nine go to heaven in a gold-mine bust'? That's what he said, and then, *boom,* their mine explodes into this big dust cloud that covers the sun."

Ramón kept going. "Anyway, he also predicted the death of this town. His last prophecy. And that's the one everybody's talking about."

"How's it go?"

"It's another poem," said Cody.

"A poem?" Cruz laughed at that. "He was a poet *and* a psychic?"

"Only after enough homemade wine," said Wil. "I forget how it goes, but there's this stranger who comes to town and he causes the death of a great man, and the whole town goes to ruin. That's what people are so worried about."

"There's one more part," said Ramón. "Supposedly, the guy who dies has a secret. And if that secret's discovered in time, the town'll be saved."

"Well, okay," said Cruz. "Now you're talking."

Cody rolled over and spun toward Tom. "Say the poem, Tom. You're the only one who knows the whole thing."

Tom, still stargazing, squeezed shut his eyes. He knew this was coming. "You guys—" He paused. "It's not that easy to remember."

But he was vastly outnumbered. They all knew he knew the poem and they all—even Frankie—demanded to hear it.

Slowly, Tom rose and sat cross-legged facing the center of their circle. His hands felt moist. His mouth was dry. "Okay," he said. "First, he always starts a prophecy with the same couplet."

"With what?" asked Wil.

"Shhh," said Cody. "It's that little poem. You know."

Tom drooped his eyes so he could wander to the back of his brain. Then he started, slow as a death march.

> *Blackjack Buck's in a wine barrel room,*
> *A barrelhouse King who sees all things.*
>
> *I see days of discord, doom, and gloom.*
> *I see a swirling wind.*

> *Under the rays of the rising sun,*
> *I see a stranger from the east ride in.*
>
> *The stranger spurs a great man's death.*
> *I see Dillontown torn asunder—*
> *Lest the dead man's secret can be learned*
> *Before the town falls prey to plunder.*
>
> *Oh, the stranger lies between lies and truth,*
> *But the truth lies here, my friends.*
> *A double-cross begins the day,*
> *And by a double loss it ends.*

For a moment a graveyard silence filled the air. Tom felt sure everyone else was now thinking what he'd been thinking ever since Cruz first appeared—that Cruz was the stranger. And that somehow—maybe even by accident—he'd cause the death of someone great.

Someone with a secret.

Cruz lowered himself back down onto his stomach, propping himself with his elbows. "Well," he said, "I'll say this. That guy's a born poet."

"Yeah?" Frankie ventured. "What else? What do you think it means?" Tom noticed his stomach tighten at the question.

Cruz hunched his shoulders. "*No sé.* But I think I do know one secret that will save this town from plunder."

"You do?"

"Yep. And Tom and I have a plan to get it. Tell 'em, Tom."

"What? What do you mean?"

"You know. Mr. Nineteen for Nineteen."

Tom's heart pounded. "I still don't know—"

"Yeah, you do." He addressed them all. "We're going to—Tom and I—we're going to ask Mr. Dante Del Gato if he'd come down here and coach our team and share his secret of hitting with us."

The other boys sent out a whooshing sound that filled the sky.

"We *are*?" said Tom. "When did we—"

Then, out of the dark came a voice.

"I think that's the best idea I've heard all day." All heads whipped sideways to see María appear out of the shadows of the pepper tree. "And here I thought you guys were idiots."

Then out popped Rachel and Tara as all three girls approached, clutching their sleeping bags against them.

"We're sleeping out here, too," María announced. "That tent's okay, but Tom, your dad snores like a dog barking backwards." She looked around. "Besides, we heard you laughing, but way over there, it's like we're not even part of the team."

"Of course you are," said Frankie. "You kidding?" He sat up and wiggled his bag to the side, as if in a kayak, scooting up against Wil to make more room. "Here, Rachel, squeeze in between me and Cody."

"Yeah, right." María tossed her bag on the ground beneath the tree. "Nice try, Pancho. But no squeeze plays. We're sleeping over here. We just don't want to be left out."

"Yeah, that's cool." Cruz rose and waved. "Hi, Rachel. Hi, Tara."

The sisters grinned, then spread their bags out past María's.

Tom sat stunned, as if in a dream. It was weird enough that both Frankie and Cruz could talk to girls as easy as they talk to boys—an astounding feat by Tom's standards. But when Cruz told everyone that Tom would help him talk to Del Gato—that idea numbed his whole body.

María settled on top of her bag. "Look," she said, "you guys just go back to scratching and belching and telling dumb jokes. Don't mind us. But remember, we're in this thing together."

"So you say it's okay," asked Wil, "if a crazy man coaches our team?"

"Desperate times," said María, "call for desperate measures. And right now, we're all desperados. But after hearing those ladies attack Mr. G today, I know they're going to blame us, too, if we don't come through. So, I'm up for taking my chances with the crazy man. I say, go for it."

She twisted around, banged her pillow, then lay back down against it. She'd only said a few words, but for Tom, they were strong, beautiful words. *We're all desperados.* We're in this together. Go for it. Who cares about a dumb ol' prophecy? Who cares if we're facing some overcoached, oversmug baseball team? And who cares if a wild girl who might sit up and talk to you at any moment is sleeping just twenty feet away?

A desperado like Tom could handle that. Right? And he only had to turn sideways to see her lying there, dressed in shorts and a T-shirt, a bent knee stuck in the air. But now, he realized, he was seeing her, *la desperada*, in a brand-new light. And it wasn't just the stars.

7

A boy needs to read the earth. This is a truth older than the iron dust that redpaints the boulders. It's older than the woolback mammoths that're fossiled in these hills. It's a feeling truth, a gut truth from deep inside, that leads a boy to bouldertops on mountaintops, scanning ancient vistas, listening like a perched hawk, reading willow trees for buried water, canyonsides for fruit or meat, and the ridgetops for friend or stranger.

It leads a boy to wander nights, to turn blind corners and enter black-eyed caves, hunting for earthen knowledge, following a starborne hunch.

Even a book boy, like Tom Gallagher, has to read the earth, this wind, that wind, and rain clouds building. Inside, he has a craving, not to be denied.

This is the truth. A boy kept distant from the earth is a boy dissatisfied.

Sometime in the dead of night, Tom felt someone shake his shoulder.

"You with me, *compadre*?" Cruz whispered.

Tom squeezed his eyes tight, gave his face a hard rub,

then slowly looked around. By now, the earth had spun toward a whole new set of stars. The quarter moon had risen higher and hung like a smile over White Fang Peak. He sat up without saying a word.

On fox feet, Cruz slipped away and headed for the barn. By the time Tom had pulled on his jeans and boots, hit the bunkhouse, splashed some water on his face, and entered the barn, Cruz had the horses saddled up and was loading his laptop into a leather pouch. "Anybody see you?" he asked.

"Cody. I told him we'd be back by breakfast, but if not, to tell my dad I took you out for a little ride."

"You're an honorable man," said Cruz.

Tom shook his head. "No, I just don't like being put on the spot."

They rode the dirt road along Doc's farm and crossed the highway by the string of mailboxes at the foot of Doc's drive. The clop of iron horseshoes on the asphalt seemed as loud as a hammer on stone. Tom glanced back toward his house and yard. He saw no movement.

Along the fence line, Tom took the lead as they rode in silence to the edge of the mayor's pastureland. Two cows stood next to the white board fence, sleeping. Tom had not ridden in so long, the saddle felt hard beneath him. He stood on his stirrups a moment and resettled. The horse huffed loudly through wide nostrils and shook his head. Tom patted his neck. The cows did not move.

As they left the highway's edge and cut into a field, the trail widened, and they rode side by side. Before long the two riders were out of the dim glow of town light and into the shadowless murk of early morning.

"How far away is it?" asked Cruz.

"About an hour."

"Tough climb?"

"The last part. It goes uphill pretty fast."

"How's your horse?"

"He'll be all right."

"What's his name?"

"Pronto."

In the tall brush, crickets scraped their wings into chirps. The tough, gangly branches of scrub oak and wild lilac bushes rose up on both sides of the trail, higher than the riders. The night sky towered over them, too, the way massive oak trees covered a canyon, letting in only sparkles of daylight—just like stars—through the leaves.

"You sure are quiet."

Tom nodded. "That's what everybody says."

"What're you thinking?"

"I don't know." Tom was happiest when he could sit silent, be the observer, the noticer of small details, the sketcher.

They rode another ten minutes or so in silence, to the foot of Rattlesnake Ridge. By now a trace of morning was breaking behind White Fang Peak, the highest point on the ridge. Cruz stopped his horse and gazed off toward the glow.

"Sure pretty," he said. "You lived out here all your life?"

"Yeah."

"Tell me about these guys. Frankie and Ramón and everybody."

Tom thought a moment. "Well, Frankie Flores is my closest friend. Known him the longest."

"I figured that."

"Yeah, he's either over at my house or I'm over at his all the time. He's a great shortstop. But he's kind of girl crazy. And María's his cousin. She's kind of—bossy."

Cruz laughed. "That's a nice word for it. She's kind of pretty, too."

That startled Tom. "You think so?"

"You don't?"

"I never thought about it." That was a lie, and Tom knew it. But it had just happened that night. Seeing María as something more than Frankie's obnoxious cousin was brand-new to him, and besides, it might all change tomorrow. So he just kept going. "And Ramón, he's smart. He's like a brainiac. In third grade he was building websites and posting time-lapse photos of the moon and stars and stuff like that."

Cruz tisked his horse into motion. "Seriously? I like guys like that."

"Yeah, me too. And he's a good outfielder." Tom remembered how he and Ramón had spent all of fourth grade building a video game called Killer Apes of Alpine, and wondered what'd happened to it. Then he continued. "And Cody, he's the youngest. And he acts like it."

"Good ballplayer?"

Tom laughed. "Better than me. And he's only eleven years old."

"So this team we're playing, they're all twelve, like us?"

"An all-star team, practically, of twelve-year-olds. Ask Wil."

"Oh, yeah, what about Wil? He's a catcher, right? Seems goofy."

"He is. But he and Ramón are our best hitters. And Wil's okay. But, like Frankie says, he's not exactly the sharpest crayon in the box."

Cruz nodded his understanding. "Rachel has some real power, I noticed. Good, quick swing. And María—she's got some pop, too. Strong shoulders, strong legs. And she's tall."

"Yeah," Tom agreed. "They both play softball. They were on all-stars and everything." The image of María's shoulders flashed into his mind. Then her long legs. And Tom could see what Cruz saw. There was something pretty about her. And strong.

"What about you?" asked Tom. "What do you like to do?"

"I'm doing it. I like to explore. Like to play ball. And when I'm not goofing off, I like to sit on the tack-shed roof and figure stuff out."

"Well, that's good. Because I hope you figured out what you're going to say to Del Gato when we get there. Because once we reach his place, you're on your own, *compadre*."

"No problem. That's all I've been thinking about lately, anyway. Whole trip out here, this video of his kept running through my head."

"What video?"

"Oh, about six months ago, I bought a tape of those last nineteen at-bats."

"You did? You bought that? So did I! Amazing, right?"

"Yeah, but did you notice something strange?"

"No—well, I mean, sure, he was perfect for five games in a row. I mean, who does that?"

"Yeah, but it's *how* he did it," said Cruz. "In all of those last nineteen at-bats, he only sees fifty-one pitches. *And* he only swings the bat nineteen times."

Tom considered that a moment. "Yeah, okay. So?"

"So that means he never swings and misses. He never even fouls one off. He swings nineteen times and hits the ball hard each time, and it never comes close to being caught by a fielder."

"I still don't see what you mean."

"What I mean is, it was like he was standing there tossing the ball up and hitting it, fungo style, anywhere he wanted the ball to go. And that's when I realized Dante Del Gato had discovered the *secret of hitting.*"

Tom jerked his head sideways. *"Secret?"* That prophetic word bounced around his brain. "You really think there's a secret to hitting?"

"Well, yeah. I mean, it's pretty obvious. There's got to be some secret, some incredible little piece of knowledge that he must've discovered at the end of his career, to pull that off."

Tom gazed hard at Cruz. "Wait a minute. You think the whole art and science of hitting a baseball can be boiled down to one little secret?"

"More than that. I think it can be figured out by guys like us."

Tom leaned both forearms against his saddle horn. He could barely keep riding. Lightning thoughts shot around his head, over the mountains and valleys of his brain. Was it possible? Could one secret method give a batter the ability to hit any kind of pitch from any pitcher he faced?

"But there's still one thing," said Cruz, "I just don't get."

"What's that?"

"Well, say Del Gato finally did learn the secret. So, okay, he's the best hitter in baseball, he's got money, women, and fame. And next stop, the World Series. So why would a guy turn his back on all that?"

They rode again in stillness. The sky had grayed slowly with the dawn, and only a few stars lingered overhead. But inside Tom's head, the wheels whirled at light speed, spinning with possibilities, pictures, and random thoughts.

He led the way, up the ridge crest, down a small ravine, and up again into the thicket. Stiff, scraggly branches of redberry and manzanita scratched against his legs. He turned sharply to avoid a stand of beavertail cactus, with its paddle-like leaves full of needles. Then he angled down alongside a huge boulder, into a clearing, and stopped.

"See that?" He pointed to several smooth depressions on top of the granite stone. "Grinding holes." He waved his arm. "This whole place is an old Kumeyaay Indian camp. There's broken pottery scattered all over." Tom swiveled in the saddle. "There's an underground spring over there by that cottonwood. And only a hundred years ago, Kumeyaay people were still living right here."

"Here?" Cruz scoped the rugged landscape. "Not much to it."

"Yeah, I know. But this was one of their camps of last

resort. See, they used to live all over the county, depending upon the season. Summers and winters, they'd head to the beaches. Each fall, they'd hike up into the mountains where the black oaks grow. The best acorns come from black oaks. But back then a lot of people from the east were moving out here. And when they saw the Indians leave, they swarmed in. They figured the Indians were moving away for good. And by the time the Kumeyaay migrated back the next season, their land was occupied."

"Oh, man," said Cruz, pointing a finger at Tom. "See? Same problem we got today. Developers."

Tom gave a small laugh. "Yeah, really. Anyway, the Indians were outnumbered, so they just kept moving back, farther and farther into the hills. Finally into dark little gulches like this. There's over fifteen thousand big and little sites like this all over San Diego. Doc's got one on his land, too."

Cruz sat up high and surveyed the small *campo* in silence.

"See that cluster of manzanita?" asked Tom. "All in rows? That's not by chance. That's an ancient garden. The berries are sweet, but you need a bunch just to make a snack."

"Ah, *las manzanas pequeñas*," said Cruz. "Yeah, I see them." He studied the twisted, glossy red branches, and beyond them, the ancient cottonwood tree, its roots drinking from the trickle of a miracle spring coming out of nowhere.

"But the best thing," said Tom, "are those big, huge trees beyond the cottonwood."

"Big-leaf maples," said Cruz. "Boy, nice size."

Tom was surprised that Cruz could name them.

"That's the kind of bat I have," said Cruz. "From a Pine Valley tree."

"No kidding? Doc made me a bat once from one of his trees. He's got a lathe in his work shed. I watched him, but I never made one myself."

"Still have it?"

"Yeah, but it's too small to use, too light. I was only ten."

"Bring it tomorrow, will you? I'd like to see it." Cruz turned back to the grinding stones. "Man, Tom. It's almost spooky up here. You feel the people, don't you? People all around us. It's like we're right in the middle of an ancient town."

"I know," said Tom, "but not for long. This place'll probably go next. Once they build out Doc's ridge with a bunch of little ten-acre 'ranchettes' and sell them for a million bucks each, they'll probably start up here."

Tom led the way out of the canyon and over the next ridge crest. "I do think my dad's right, though," he said. "That our town's dying. But if this deal's the right way to save it, why's it feel so wrong? Know what I mean?"

"I do." Cruz caught up to Tom now that they rode the south wall of the canyon and the brush had thinned. "When I was ten my dad told me something I think about a lot. Back when he was dying from cancer and he knew I was going to be taking over the business, he said, 'When you have a tough decision to make, listen to your gut feeling. To that tiny voice down inside.' And he said that the fastest way to lose touch with that voice was by being greedy."

Tom said nothing—he couldn't think of anything good enough to say. But he felt an admiration now for Cruz and his dad that gave him a good gut feeling.

"You know what else is dying?" said Cruz. "Baseball."

Tom looked at him and grinned. "No way. Baseball will never die. You mean because of the players' strikes and high salaries and everything?"

"Oh, well, maybe, but I'm talking about another problem baseball has. A huge one that I figure could kill the game off entirely."

"What?"

Cruz looked side to side and behind him, then said softly, "Tee ball."

"Tee ball? What're you talking about?"

Cruz gave an openmouthed grin. "It's true. Tee ball is killing baseball. First realized it when I saw those games they had on the White House lawn."

"That was just a bunch of little kids running around having fun."

"To you, maybe. But to me, I saw something else. See, tee ball is a game that old people invented. And why? Because little kids don't pitch or hit all that well. So they eliminated pitching and turned hitting into golf."

Tom considered the idea a moment. "Yeah. So?"

"So they're killing baseball and they don't even know it. They're killing the ability of kids to learn the most important part of the game—to follow a ball with their eyes. And to swing and hit a moving target. If you don't learn that when you're little, you'll never learn it very well—at least you'll never learn to hit Major League pitching when you get older."

"Why not?"

"When I was watching all those tapes of Del Gato, I realized a good hitter reads the pitch. He decodes it and interprets it. Then he speaks to it."

"What?"

"Yeah, really. I figured out that learning to hit a baseball is like learning a foreign language. If you want to speak a foreign language without an accent, you have to do it when you're young. After a certain age, it's too late. Same with hitting."

"Keep talking."

"Well, I was sitting there watching that tee ball game when it hit me that Del Gato was doing the same thing."

"Playing tee ball?"

"Well, yeah, sort of. It was like, after all these years, he could now hit a Major League fastball like it was sitting on a tee. And so I asked myself: If tee ball is where you want to end up, then where should you begin? What's the secret?"

Tom had no answer for that. He glanced at Cruz, who shrugged, saying, "I'm not a hundred percent sure, but I think I'm close to figuring it out."

Tom stood up in his stirrups. "You're serious, aren't you?"

"Serious as a diamondback in your boot." Cruz raised an eyebrow. "That's why we're going to Del Gato's. And that's where you come in, my friend." Then he kicked his horse and rode off ahead.

As they reached the base of White Fang Peak, Tom lifted his hat and wiped his forehead. He looked at his watch. Not yet six o'clock and the morning was already warm. In the distance, he could hear cars on the highway, workers making the thirty-five-mile commute into San Diego.

They stood their horses, gazing up over the thick growth of manzanita shrubs mingled with leather-leafed sugar bush climbing to the top of the hill.

"Can't even see his house from here, can you?" asked Cruz.

"You'd need a helicopter. But the gate comes first, about halfway up. And I'm sure it's locked."

Cruz kept staring at the hill.

"Besides that," Tom added, "there's a ten-foot-high wall around the place, with sharp iron rods on top."

Cruz looked at him and grinned. "No high-voltage electricity?" He paused a moment to read the mountain, then tisked his horse and set off. He did not take the driveway that twisted its way to the gate. Instead, he rode through the brush. "Looks like a straighter shot," he called.

Tom valued that ability, reading a mountain by its brush-tops and figuring out a trail even though the ground itself was impossible to see. To him it came naturally, he'd done it all his life, but he didn't know many others who could do it.

As they stepped, the horses stirred up rabbits and quail from out of the brush, but neither horse spooked. Seemed to be their natural terrain as well.

"What if he's not up yet?" asked Tom.

"We'll throw rocks at his front door." Cruz ran Screwball down and up a small erosion ditch.

"Or we can wait," Tom called after him. "We've got plenty of time before we have to get back."

Now a bit alarmed that Cruz was acting overconfident, Tom added, "People say he shoots trespassers."

This time Cruz slowed and gave Tom a serious glance. "We're not trespassers. We're here on a mission from God." Then he tisked again and rustled the reins as Screwball scampered ahead.

A quarter mile up the hill, they passed two posts with signs painted in big red letters: NO TRESPASSING! KEEP OFF!

Cruz rode on past. Tom sat still a moment, then took a big breath and slowly moved forward. Near the hilltop, the riders rejoined the paved driveway at its final switchback before one last steep climb.

Within a few yards of the gate, Cruz glanced back. "That's a tall fence," he said. Tom fought a serious urge to turn around and head on home. Cruz slid off his horse.

Nothing about the old stucco wall with its black iron spikes, nor the iron gate showing the dense, tree-filled compound inside, seemed all that welcoming to Tom.

Cruz studied the adobe brick columns abutting the entryway. "Is there a bell or an intercom or something?"

Tom lifted his shoulders. "Never been this close before."

Cruz stepped up, grasped the bars, and leaned in, scanning the grounds. "Okay," he said. "I got a plan."

Inside Tom's gut, a cluster of startled snakes rattled a warning.

Cruz wiggled his hand. "What I need is a—a—" He made a fist. "Like a hook or something."

"A hook?" Tom looked into the forest of treetops above the wall. Orange, apple, avocado, eucalyptus. "You're going fishing?" He stayed atop Pronto, who circled once, lifting skittery hooves.

"No, a *big* hook. Like a claw. I need some metal or something." He began walking along the base of the wall, scanning the ground.

Tom hopped down to help. Leading Pronto, he walked in the other direction, circling the compound, but found nothing worthwhile by the time he met up with Cruz on the other side. "Only metal I saw," said Tom, "was a couple of beer cans and a few short, rusty pieces of old iron rods that've probably been there since they built this wall." He bit down on a smile. Now Cruz would have to forget whatever crazy scheme he had in mind.

"You mean like these?" Out of his back pocket, Cruz pulled three iron rods about ten inches long.

Tom laughed. "Yeah, but what are you going to do, bend them with your bare hands?"

"No, I got an idea. Listen. Go back and pick up all those beer cans, okay? I'll meet you over by the gate."

Tom found five aluminum cans and dumped them on the pile Cruz had already made with his own find.

"More than enough," said Cruz. He pulled out his pocket-knife and began sawing off the bottoms of each can. "That's where the toughest metal is," he said. "On the ends."

He took six silver bottoms and, with his knife, pierced each one through the middle.

"What're you going to do?"

"Hang on. You'll see." Cruz placed the round bottoms on the ground, like a stack of poker chips about an inch high. Through the stack he rammed the three iron rods, one at a time, so he ended up with something that looked like an upside-down three-legged stool.

"Tom, I need the rope off my saddle."

Tom hustled away and brought back the coil of rope. "I still don't see what you're doing," he said.

Cruz untied the leather lash that bundled the rope. He used the lash to tie the rods tightly together, right where they met above the base. Then he spread the three "legs" even more, as if making a tiny teepee. Finally, he wound the end of his rope around the base and through it several times, securing the metal "chips" to each other and holding the rods in place.

He stood and pulled out more rope. The metal contraption dangled in front of him, rods up, looking more like a three-fingered claw than a hook.

Cruz whirled it around and around. *"Excelente!"*

He turned, grabbed his hat, and smiled at Tom. "Now I'm going to snag me that oak tree I saw around back, growing just inside his wall. Then I'm going in."

"You're crazy. You're going to get halfway up that wall,

then that thing's going to come flying apart, and you'll land on your butt like some dumb rodeo rider getting tossed off a bull."

Cruz didn't look at him. He inspected his homemade grappling hook and said, "No, I think it'll work." He started off, leaving Tom to follow, leading both horses.

"But what about the dogs? He's got man-eating dogs. That's not a legend. It's true!"

Cruz turned his ear toward the wall. "Don't hear anything. Maybe you got it wrong, Tom. Maybe somebody saw a man *eating* dogs." He raised a finger. "Now, that might be true."

On the far side of the property, the morning sun lit the whitewashed wall and the upper branches of the gangly oak in Del Gato's backyard. Tom tied the horses to a sprawling sumac bush not far away. Meanwhile, Cruz slipped on a pair of leather batting gloves he'd pulled from his bag, then hopped up on a small granite boulder nearby. Slowly, he began to twirl the rope.

Tom kept his distance behind and to the side of Cruz, just in case something went flying off.

"It'll be just like rock climbing," said Cruz. "Like going up the face of a ten-foot boulder." He spun the contraption in wider, faster loops. "Nothing to it."

The claw took off through the air, into the leaves and branches of the tree. Neither boy could see where it landed, but it didn't matter. Cruz yanked, the line jerked back, gave a little, then caught. He yanked again, and this time it held firm. The line ran from the tree, over the wall, then down to Cruz's hands. He pulled once more and leaned back so far his hat fell off, but the rope didn't give an inch.

It was ready. "Give me a boost, Tom."

Tom could not move. Now that same cluster of snakes was not only rattling at full fury, they had crawled into his arms and legs.

"Come on, Tom." Cruz grabbed his hat, shoved it on. "Either give me a boost or bring me my horse."

Finally, Tom approached. He decided that all he had to do was to give him a boost, then hide behind the wall, safe and sound. Sure, he thought, this won't be so bad. He threaded his fingers together and set them under Cruz's dusty boot. "Ready?"

Without a word, Cruz stepped up onto Tom's hands, bent his knees, and put a foot against the wall. He grabbed high on the rope, brought his other foot around, and began walking up the wall.

Tom barely moved from underneath. He's really doing it, he thought. This guy is crazy.

"I'll stay here," Tom said, "in case I need to break your fall."

Cruz was breathing too hard to answer. He just kept going, a cowboy Spider-Man lurching up a wall.

Then it happened.

Just as Cruz reached the very top, he squatted and yanked with all his might. Tom heard a crack. And before he knew what to make of that, a giant section of wall tore loose and crashed into Del Gato's backyard. Like a surfing *vaquero*, Cruz rode a huge chunk of Spanish stucco straight into the wild unknown.

In the echo of the boom, through the dust and gloom, they heard a dog bark. And then another.

Come on, man! Let's go!" Tom bolted for his horse, jumping a small bush, slipping, and falling to the ground. "Come *on*!"

He got up, stumbled toward Pronto, reached out, and began untying the reins. All he could think was *man-eating dogs*—on the loose!

Finally, he yanked the reins free, backed up, stuck his left foot in the stirrup, and jumped on board.

Atop the saddle, he glanced back at the six-foot opening in Del Gato's wall. No gun barrels yet. No dogs, though he could hear them close by. All he saw was Cruz, still standing on the broken slab, holding out his hand.

"Cruz!" he shouted. "C'mon! Hurry up!"

Then he saw them. Two huge black dogs, growling, snapping out barks. They darted nervously back and forth in front of Cruz, who was softly talking to them. Slowly the dogs approached Cruz's outstretched hand. They began sniffing, then licking the back of his fist.

Tom could not believe it.

"Trina! Taco!" came a deep, booming voice. "Hold!"

Trina and Taco were not going anywhere, Tom could see. They were now receiving scratches and pats from the strange invader who had busted down their barrier to the outside world.

Then the man appeared—with a shotgun across his chest. "Hold it right there," he said to Cruz.

Tom cringed, looking for a bush to jump into, wishing he and Cruz were a million miles away, wishing he had never agreed to take him on this stupid trip. And hoping that they were not about to die.

He watched, still frozen. He imagined riding off, getting help, but he could not imagine leaving Cruz. Slowly, Tom dropped down off his horse. Standing on weak knees, he took a big breath and retied Pronto's reins to the sumac branch. Then he started walking toward the end of his life.

"I'm sorry," said Cruz, looking up at the rifleman. "I'm real sorry, I didn't mean to break your wall. I was just trying to climb over and see you. We looked for a doorbell or something."

Now Tom could see Del Gato's face, beard-stubbled and dark. So much older than in the glossy poster he had taped to his closet door at home. The face was thinner, with deeper lines down the cheeks. His hair ragged and longer, over his ears. But still, no doubt, it was him. Here was Tom's most treasured baseball card come to life, the five-time all-star, the greatest hitter in the modern era, the crazy man.

He was not tall. That surprised Tom. But he was huge, the way a ninety-five-pound mountain lion is huge, with dark, sunken, hidden-camera eyes that seemed to bullet around in his skull, shooting quick snapshots of everything in front of him.

Now they shot at Tom as he crept up to the hole in the wall. His heart pounded against his throat and chest, making it hard for him to breathe.

Cruz motioned toward the wall. "I'm really sorry about this."

"Shut up!" Del Gato pointed with his rifle. "Just stay there and keep your mouth shut." He peered up at the braided nylon rope running from the wall, over the tree, and down to where the hook was wedged between the trunk and a branch.

He said nothing, stepping past Cruz and running his hand along the jagged sections of torn adobe. The interior of the wall, now exposed along the edges of the break, had pieces of straw poking out of the brown clay.

Glancing left and right, he looked at the horses for a long moment, then turned around. With a jerk of his head, he motioned for Tom to come inside and join Cruz. Tom obliged.

"You boys came up here on horseback?"

They nodded.

Del Gato raised an eyebrow. "What in the Hail Mary were you trying to do?"

Tom looked at Cruz as if to say, "You tell him. It was your idiotic idea," though his real message was, "I can't talk. I can't even breathe."

Cruz started talking at light speed. "I'll fix it. I promise. I wasn't trying to wreck anything. I'm really sorry. I was just— I was just trying to come and see you. I've been wanting to talk to you for, like, forever. I wasn't going to break in. I was going to knock on your door. But I didn't know how else to get there. I'm sorry, I'll put it all back together. Block by block. I can stucco. I've done it before. I can—"

"Hey!" Del Gato raised his chin. "Knock it off! I didn't ask for your life story." He walked closer. "What's your name?"

"Cruz de la Cruz. I live in Paloma. That's Tom Gallagher. He lives here. His dad's a teacher at Scrub Oak, and his mom's the school librarian."

What a weird thing to say, thought Tom.

Del Gato lowered the shotgun and studied Tom a moment. He walked back to the oak tree, reached up, and grabbed the iron claw. He pulled it free and turned it over in his hand.

He glanced back at Cruz. "And you made this?"

"Yeah."

Del Gato examined it again, then dropped it onto the carpet of dried leaves. Without looking back, he began walking away. "Come up to the house," he growled. "I'll give you five minutes."

10

Tom had never seen a place like this. There were stone walls terracing down one side of the yard, each level full of huge fruit trees—peach, apple, avocado, nectarine. He saw vegetable gardens in raised beds of concrete block with bright yellow squash blossoms and fat red tomatoes spilling over onto the straw pathways below. Corn silk dangled from green ears, thick as bat barrels, filling the stalks.

Cruz looked back at Tom with the hint of a smile, as if to say, "Hey, some entrance, huh, *compadre*?"

Real funny, thought Tom as they walked into an open courtyard of adobe tile where purple bougainvillea bushes exploded against the house and onto the roof. Prickly pear cactus pads, loaded with cherry-red fruit, grew below and around the windows of the white Spanish stucco house. Overhead, big bunches of purple grapes hung down through redwood lattice. The grape leaves shaded four unpainted picnic tables with plank-top benches that seemed to be set out waiting for a family gathering. Chickens and ducks ran free, pecking at bugs and scattered grain, cackling and quacking, paying no notice to the dogs.

Del Gato stopped and pointed at the table closest to the house. "Have a seat." He continued on, pausing at the back doorstep. "You boys stand a cup of coffee?"

Coffee? Tom had never been offered a cup of coffee before.

"Yes, thank you," said Cruz. "Black."

"Um, yeah, me, too. Please." Then Tom muttered, "I mean, thank you."

Del Gato hung his rifle on a peg by the door and went inside. An old brown hen scuttled under the table, flapped its wings, and chased off another bird.

Tom whispered behind his hand. "Why'd you tell him about my mom and dad?"

Cruz whispered back. "I had to think fast. I figured maybe they all grew up together or something." He shrugged. "Just a gut feeling."

"No way. Dad's from Anaheim. And Mom's too young."

"Okay, man, but still, you're his homeboy. Be good if you could soften him up. You know, you're from the same school, play at the same ballpark he did. Whatever you can think of."

Tom squirmed. "I'm not good at that!"

Del Gato kicked open the door holding three cups and a chipped white enamel coffeepot. Chickens and ducks scattered as he stepped down and poured the coffee, then sat in a redwood chair at the end of the table.

"So you're Helen's boy."

Tom froze, mouth open. He tried to nod.

"How's she doing?"

"F-fine."

"And your old man? How's he getting along?"

Tom took a short breath. "Same as always, I guess."

Del Gato moved his eyes from Tom to Cruz, then breathed out his nose like a bull. "So what do you boys want?"

Cruz glanced over and lifted his chin at Tom with expectant eyes.

Me? thought Tom. Are you insane? Tom's eyes were so wide, he felt that if he leaned forward, they'd fall out. Eyes that said, "Don't you know anything about me yet?" Words swirled inside his head as if they were caught going around a giant toilet bowl while Tom tried to fish one—any one— out. He felt a chicken peck at the toe of his boot.

Finally, Cruz stepped in as a pinch hitter.

"Well, you see," he started. "The mayor and a few other guys want to put in this building project. And they talked Doc Altenheimer into going along with it."

"The mayor? That double-crossing sack of cow's cud. He's as crooked as a snake in a rake."

Tom pulled his coffee cup closer as Cruz swung away. Over a strong, bitter, boiling-hot brew, Cruz told Del Gato about the ranchettes, the golf course, the Master Plan, and the Big Game. Del Gato listened, his narrowed eyes staring at Cruz through the steam rising out of his mug.

"And finally," Cruz continued, "they want to turn the Lucky Strike into a lake." He paused like an actor. "Unless we win that ball game. If we can beat those guys, the deal's off."

"Whose dumb idea was that? The mayor's?"

"No," said Cruz. "It was—well, Doc's, sort of. I mean, actually I guess Tom here kind of gave him the idea."

Del Gato angled a glance at Tom. Then, slow as sunrise, he sent him a grin. "You did, huh? You figure your team can beat that squad?"

Tom's head shook. "N-not really." His wind was almost

gone. "Doc just thought that the only way we could ever be any good is if we had all that brand-new stuff. But I . . ." His breath was gone.

With a rugged hand, Del Gato gave his mouth and chin a dry shave. Even from where Tom sat, he could hear the scratch of beard stubble. The chicken pecked harder at his toes, and Tom had to shift his feet, then gently boot the pesky bird sideways, sending it *bawk-bawk*ing into the flower bed.

Del Gato sat back and crossed his arms. "And in your great wisdom, you boys thought that I would be overjoyed to come down and coach your team. That I'd give a damp duck whether they bury this town or not."

Now the old chicken ran up and over Del Gato's outstretched legs as it chased away two smaller birds from a corncob.

"Yeah," said Cruz. "That's what we thought."

Del Gato grabbed the pot handle and poured himself another splash. "Drown the ball field, huh?"

Tom sipped his coffee. He hated the taste, but he didn't know what else to do.

Del Gato reached down and caught the pesky hen by its head—just clamped his leathery fist down over its head, picked the bird up by the neck, and swung its body around like Cruz had swung his iron hook.

With a crack, the neck bone snapped. The chicken's wings flapped and fluttered a few times, and Del Gato swung again until it stopped.

He held the limp chicken a couple moments longer, then

dropped it on the table next to the coffeepot. "Well," he said, "there's my answer."

Tom's heart galloped. He tried to process what he'd just seen.

Del Gato gulped his coffee, lowered the mug, and swirled the grounds, tossing them into the flower bed. He stood. "I don't leave the *rancho* much." He glanced out toward a cluster of fruit trees. "Got just about all I need. Grow my own food. If I want chicken dinner, I walk out and here it is. And one thing I don't need is any more aggravation." He lowered his voice. "You hear me?"

Both boys studied their coffee.

Del Gato walked to an old brick fireplace and threw in a bunch of twigs and branches. He grabbed a red can and splashed the wood with whatever was inside. Next, he opened a spigot and ran water from a hose into a black iron kettle. While it filled, he lit a match and tossed it into the pit. With a whoosh, flames rose as high as the grape leaves, then settled. The firewood crackled and spat.

Tom swung his legs over the bench and stood, ready to go. Ready to run like crazy. Cruz barely moved. He took another swallow, set the cup down. "Just one more thing, Mr. Del Gato," he said. "If I could."

Del Gato froze a moment, then stirred the flame.

Cruz went on. "At the end of your career, it seems to me you discovered something about hitting. Something really big. And I'm just wondering if I discovered the same thing."

Del Gato placed an old greasy grill across two brick

ledges just above the fire, turned off the water, then set the kettle on the grill.

"I got a chicken to pluck." He waved his hand, dismissing them. "You boys can go out the way you came in. And this time, don't wreck anything."

11

I really didn't think he'd be like that," said Cruz after he and Tom had ridden partway down the mountain. "I expected him to be some kind of weirdo." He grinned and reached out to slap Tom's shoulder with his hat.

"Yeah, I know," said Tom. "He didn't even wear a hockey mask."

Cruz wiped his forehead, then pulled his hat back on. "Of course, we shouldn't be too hard on the guy. I'm sure he wasn't expecting anybody to be *dropping* in."

"Nah," said Tom, riding farther into the brush. "And he's probably lonely. Next time, let's knock down his front gate and stay for lunch. He's got to be a great cook. Tell by his coffee."

"Coffee? Thought that was boiled chicken blood."

From there, they took a long, quiet ride back to camp, arriving just before nine. Quickly they fed the horses, then changed into their gear.

"You know," said Tom. "I say we dodged a bullet—literally. I mean, can you imagine what kind of coach he'd be? If we'd stuck around there any longer, we'd probably've ended up like that chicken." They crossed the yard as Tom continued. "But what was that you told him at the end? About hitting and discovering what he did. What does that mean?"

"Means, I think there really is a way to conquer hitting.

And I wish I could've shown him my idea and compared it to what he did."

"What idea?"

"Oh, yeah, I started to tell you. I developed a little video game to improve my hitting. And I think I'm getting it close to being perfect. Some days, when I stand up to bat, I can see the ball coming like it's in slow motion. And on those days, I hit like a superstar. Like I'm Dante Del Gato."

The workouts on Tuesday morning were nothing like Monday's. Mr. and Mrs. Gallagher dreamed up a drill they called, "Eight/Four, Hit, Run, Score." While four players batted, eight players, including Mr. and Mrs. Gallagher, would scatter around the field playing defense.

The four-player team would hit until they had six outs against them. Then a new team of four would rotate in.

"I'll pitch to the first bunch," said Mr. Gallagher. "Then, Cruz, I want you to pitch to the next group. You seem to have a pretty live arm."

Cruz nodded, and the drill began.

But even with Tom's dad pitching, the hitting results were not hopeful. "We need serious help," Frankie told Tom. "Tara can't hit anything out of the infield. Clifford's late on half his swings. Cruz was the only one connecting."

Just as the first group rotated out, the distant sound of drums and horns filled the morning air.

"Oh, no," said Rachel. "Here they come again."

Over the small ridge and down the bank came The

Band, behind a big banner that read, DILLONTOWN
WILDSCAT! GO FOR THE GOLD!!

"They can't even spell our name right," said Tara.

"And," Frankie observed, "there's more of them today than
yesterday."

María agreed. "I guess being pathetic is contagious."

"If it is," said Wil, "they probably caught it from us."

*Boom-lay, boom-lay, boom-boom-boom. Boom-lay, boom-lay,
boom. Ba-boom.*

Today the old pipe-smoking men from the town plaza had
joined the march, along with Hollis B, who crouched off to
the side, again reporting the event to the universe. Even Doc
had wandered down and across his lower pasture to see what
was going on. Tom spotted him sitting in his usual seat, on
the top row of the stands, leaning against the back wall.

Mr. Gallagher called to the team. "Okay, everyone, back to
work! Let's stay focused. This is good for us, getting used to
playing in front of a bunch of fans."

"That's right," added Mrs. Gallagher. "Let their enthusiasm inspire you."

Cruz began warming up. "I just hope they brought the
food."

"Food?" Wil hung his head. "Dude, we need more than
food. You know what I heard this morning? Now they got
Sean Lemanski on their team. He's a pitcher from El Cajon.
I asked my dad to call and see if he could play for us."

"Is he good?" asked Tom.

"Good? He's murder. He was in our winter ball league.

Nobody could hit him. So we need more than tacos, man. We need a miracle."

As Tom jogged out to right field, he noticed the buzz among the fans was louder today. More excitement. Approaching the stone wall, he caught a glint of sunlight off the windshield of an old battered pickup rolling slowly up the dirt lane just beyond the wall. Heading straight past him.

When he saw the driver, Tom's poor stomach flopped like a chicken on a tabletop. It was the crazy man, Dante Del Gato.

Oh, no, thought Tom. The wall! He's here to tell my parents what we did. Tom kept watching as the former ballplayer drove his squeaky truck on by, skirting the outfield and finally parking in the dirt lot behind third base.

There he stepped out, walked toward the field, through the crazy band, and into a frozen silence.

No one, not even Hollis B, said a word. Del Gato walked to the gate near the dugout, eyeing the diamond, eyeing the players, with the eyes of a mountain lion. He did not enter the field, but stood at its edge, as if sniffing the wind for trouble.

Mrs. Gallagher stepped forward. "Hello, Dante," she called from second base. "Long time no see. May I help you?"

Tom's mouth fell open.

Del Gato stood a moment, then placed his scruffy, chicken-swinging, neck-wringing hands along the fence top, and leaned forward.

"I was just about to ask you the same thing."

This was a miracle.

Dante Del Gato prowled the field, watching, observing the players for half an hour while Cruz threw batting practice. The Gallaghers had welcomed him like a lost brother, not concerned at all by his bloodstained, faded jeans, by his scraggle-bearded jawline, nor his squint-eyed way of lasering right through anyone who happened to look his way.

Out in the field, however, the players had their doubts. "I wonder," asked Rachel, "when was the last time this guy even *saw* a baseball?"

"That doesn't bother me," said Frankie. "I'm wondering when's the last time he saw a *human being*. Before this morning, that is."

Tom had no answer to that. But what he wanted to know was when Del Gato had last seen his mom and dad. And how well did they know each other?

As he walked up and met the players spread around the field, Del Gato asked them their names, their best positions, then said to each one, "Show me a red-tailed hawk."

When Ramón turned immediately and pointed one out, hovering in a thermal updraft over Doc's field, Del Gato stood for a moment, then managed a small grin. When Tara frowned and said, "I don't even know what a hawk looks like. Birds are birds," he got impatient, turned and spat. But soon, every player knew that there were three red-tailed hawks in the surrounding eucalyptus trees, each in its own domain.

"Why was he asking us about hawks?" Rachel wondered. "What's that have to do with anything?"

Tom shrugged. "I don't know. Eyesight, maybe."

Wil shook his head and walked off. "He's a full-blown, full-grown lunatic. That's all I got to say."

Cruz pitched great batting practice that morning, throwing consistent strikes, sometimes even letting the batter know what pitch was coming next to give everyone a chance to hit.

"Inside!" he'd call, and the ball would kiss the inside corner of home plate. "Up and away!" meant the ball would arrive chest high on the outside part of the plate. "Downtown" pitches were the best. They split the plate, slow and straight, like a train pulling into the Campo depot.

Just before lunch, Del Gato asked if he could run the last drill.

"Of course," said Mr. Gallagher. "You have free rein here. We'd love it."

Del Gato waved everyone close. "Look, I'm not a coach," he stated. "I'm a ballplayer. Big difference. But as long as I'm here, I want to show you something I think's the most important thing I ever learned."

He scanned their faces. "Baseball is a game of anticipation, looking ahead at possibilities, trying to predict the future. On any pitch, anything might happen. Your job is to anticipate. To look ahead. And be ready."

He turned and gave the small mountain beyond right field a glance and a nod. "And I learned to do that right up there." He began to walk. "Let's go."

Soon, a line of ten campers, one teacher, and one school librarian followed the age-cracked leather boots of an unshaven bearcat with a bat on his shoulder through the chest-high brush and up the mountain.

He led them to a clearing near the crest of the hill and stopped. "Looks about right."

"Right for what?" asked María. "Smashing rattlesnakes with a bat?"

Tom glanced around. Sagebrush and greasewood filled this side—the west side—of the mountain, growing between scattered boulders. Give him fifty years, and Tom would not be able to figure out why the players were standing here.

Del Gato stared down the mountain, over the top of the rugged chaparral. "See your ball field down there?"

They could all glimpse an edge of the diamond below.

"There's no trails between here and there except what the rabbits and deer and coyotes have cut for themselves. What I want you to do is to take off running, one after the other, down the mountain. There's only one rule. Don't stop. That means if you have to cut and switch direction to avoid rocks and ditches, fine. Do what you have to do to make it down. Just don't stop running. And we'll all meet up again at second base."

Mr. Gallagher cleared his throat. "Uh, Dante, I'm a bit uncomfortable with this. It's pretty rough terrain. We don't want anyone spraining an ankle or twisting a knee. Besides, this mountain is fragile native habitat."

Del Gato raised his eyebrows. "Who told you that?"

Tom's dad gave a quick laugh. "Well," he started, and folded his arms. "I teach about these plants all year long. Chaparral vegetation exists no place else on earth, and it's the fastest disappearing native habitat on the planet. We need to preserve any little spot that's left."

Del Gato blew out his breath. "Yeah, well, I heard that preserving habitat is what this Big Game's all about. Reason I'm here."

Mr. Gallagher eyed his wife, and she gave him a slight smile.

Del Gato lost patience. "Look, you want me to help or not?"

"Well, of course, but not if—"

"Then let the kids run, for cripe sakes. Listen, you told me I had free rein. Fine. If this team's supposed to be ready by Saturday, then we've got to jack things up a notch. And I can tell by looking, these kids need it."

Not a single player moved. Tom wanted to disappear behind the nearest rock. Mr. Gallagher stood rubbing the back of his neck, but before he could manage a response, Tom's mother took a step forward.

"What if I go first?" she said, giving Tom's dad a glance. "I'll see what it's like, Jerry, then we'll have a better feel for it." She placed a hand on Del Gato's arm.

He stared right at her, slowly pinched his mouth into half a grin, and said, "Knock yourself out, Helen." He stood back and waved her along.

That is not my mom, thought Tom. That's not the quiet,

book-stacking, fact-finding media librarian I know. And she touched Del Gato!

Tom watched her start out, a bend in her knees, tennis shoes slipping as she wove her way past gopher holes, green brush, and volcanic rock, slowly at first, then picking up speed. Before long she was halfway down. Tom's dad turned and nodded at Del Gato, who tapped Ramón on the shoulder. "Go!" he said. Then he touched Frankie's shoulder. "Go!"

They both took off running.

Then Cruz, Rachel, Cody, and the rest. One by one he sent them all down. Even Mr. Gallagher.

Like his mom, Tom started off slowly, too. He had run through brush in shorter bursts, but never down a mountain nonstop. The hard part was not being able to stop. Sure, he could read the brushtops, as he'd done for years, sensing a trail that he couldn't really see. But never at high speed.

Tom preferred pausing and ducking, looking under sumac branches for lion tracks or deer nests. Any spread of prickly pear cactus always caught his eye as a possible Spanish ruin he'd have to investigate.

At one point, he came to a dead end, blocked by a boulder and thick brush. Realizing his problem too late, he ran straight at the rock, stepped up, and grabbed a small ledge. He used his momentum to carry him up, only to discover more brush below. He leapt it without stopping, landing in a dirt clearing, tumbling once, bouncing into a greasewood bush, then rolling over. The clearing was an anthill. As if on fire, Tom hopped up and brushed red ants off his arms and neck. But once free, he did linger a moment to scan for horny toad lizards, who love to eat ants for lunch. Finding none, he took off.

After that, Tom realized he had to look farther ahead. Running down a hill was a new skill. He had to factor in his momentum, that he couldn't stop at will. He had to read the trail and see danger and escape routes before he got there. How this drill would transfer to baseball, he had no clue. But he did know he loved the sensation of "falling" down a hillside, of slip-sliding along, solving puzzle after puzzle while thinking on his feet.

From all over the mountain, hoots and screams pierced the air like hawk squeals, and the valley echoed with the clopping of cross-trainers and cleats on the hard-packed earth.

The winner? Cruz, of course. The boy who could spy a fastball speeding his way and see it in his mind like it was standing still.

At lunchtime, Tom made himself a quick *carnitas* burrito, told his mom he was going to check on the horses, and left.

Forty-five minutes later, Mrs. Gallagher found him in the bunkhouse under a bare lightbulb, scratching away in his Dreamsketcher.

She knocked on the wall.

"May I come in?"

Tom was running, still running, down the mountain, with María alongside, laughing, squeezing past in the brush—is that why they call it brush? Tom finished the sentence he was working on, then closed the book. "Sure."

Mrs. Gallagher seemed uneasy, her eyes darting about the room as if checking to be sure no one else was near. "Tom," she began, "there are a lot of stories and rumors about Mr. Del Gato. I know you know that. And I also know you admire what he accomplished as a ballplayer. But now that he's no longer just a poster on your wall, there's something I need to tell you."

Tom wiggled in his chair, head bent, avoiding his mother's eyes.

"Mom, look, if this story has to do with, uh, with you and him hooking up back in the old days or something, really, I don't want to hear about it."

Mrs. Gallagher's eyes opened wide. "Oh, my, no."

"Hear about what?" Cruz burst through the bunkhouse door and began attacking his bag on the pinewood tabletop. "Oh, hi, Mrs. G. Sorry. I need my resin bag. I'm going to pitch."

Mrs. Gallagher stood, still smiling. "Not at all, Cruz. I was just telling Tom that—that Mr. Del Gato may be grizzled and gruff on the outside, but inside, he has the tender heart of a schoolboy."

Cruz looked up. "Yeah, that's right, he does. Inside a pickle jar by his kitchen window." With that, Cruz grinned, slapped the resin bag against his palm, and in a cloud of white dust, disappeared.

Alone again, Tom's mother continued. "I know his training methods are unorthodox, but he has good intentions. He really loves baseball and this ballpark, Tom. They both mean a lot to him."

"I don't mind his methods," said Tom. "I think they're cool." He waited. "That all you wanted to tell me?"

She paced to the door, then walked back and sat next to him. "A little bit more." She rubbed her palms down the legs of her jeans. Then she began. "One night, years ago, before you were born, something happened. Something wild, scary, and wonderful."

Tom hunched forward, crossing his arms over his knees, fearing—but also looking forward to—what he was about to hear.

"It was October. Pronto was just barely two years old, and we were out riding along Rattlesnake Ridge. I'd never taken him so far from home, but it was such a beautiful afternoon, kind of blustery, but humid and warm. Then, before I knew it, huge, black thunderclouds had piled up against Kwee-A-Mak Mountain, and it started to rain. Then there was a huge thunderclap, and Pronto spooked and took off at full gallop down into a side canyon, and I couldn't stop him.

"The rain came harder, and we were flying along through what seemed like buckets of water. Then a lightning bolt struck a tree right next to us, and Pronto stumbled and fell, and I slipped off and hit my head.

"The next thing I remember, a man was gathering me up in his arms, in the black of night. The wind and rain were still roaring, but somehow he'd found Pronto and managed to load me onto him and take us to Doc's place, where Doc called your father. And I just collapsed."

"And that guy was Mr. Del Gato?"

She nodded.

"So that's how you know him?"

"Yes."

"How come you never told me this before? Mom, he's a hero! He saved your life. People should know."

"You're right. They should. Jerry and I talked about it— back then, we'd just graduated from college—and many times over the years I wished we had let the whole world know. But it wasn't up to us."

"I don't understand. Why not?"

"Well, it was a little complicated." She pulled him close. "That's really all I can say."

• • •

After lunch, Tom's dad assembled the team in the dugout and announced a new strategy. "We've decided that the best thing we can do to win the Big Game is to assign each of you a specific role. That is, a specific position in the field and in the batting order. Normally we wouldn't do that. We'd prefer that you experience all positions. But this will be like an all-star game, and we need to maximize each player's contribution to the team."

"We're all spokes in the wheel," Mrs. Gallagher added. "We all depend on each other." She gave Tom a quick wink.

Mr. Gallagher crossed in front of the dugout, tapping his pencil against his shorts. "And on that note, we've decided that Mr. Del Gato will be the manager of this team. Helen and I will assist him any way we can."

Del Gato strode forward, staring down at the players on the bench. "You've got four days," he said. "If you're our lead-off hitter, then you've got four days to learn all you can about the duties of someone who bats at the top of the order. If you're our center fielder, four days to become the best center fielder in that game on Saturday. And so on down the line."

Then he paused until his eyes connected with all twenty eyeballs inside the dugout. "I spent fourteen years in the majors, and I'm here to tell you, there are no secrets."

Tom raised his eyebrows at Cruz, who looked away, twisting his mouth the way a batter does when he disagrees with the umpire's call.

"There's no magic wand I can wave," Del Gato continued, "to turn you into great ballplayers overnight. We'll simply drill on fundamentals. Everything from hitting your cutoff man to running to first base on a dropped third strike. It'll be ground ball after ground ball, pitch after pitch, solid swing after solid swing. Until every motion becomes second nature."

Tom loved hearing that. The idea of making baseball a part of his nature stirred him up. And remembering the little things, like running on a dropped third strike, was so important. Wow, he thought. This guy might really be a great coach.

"First thing we have to do is flush those batting tees down the toilet. You kids are too young for them."

"Too young?" said Frankie.

"Your brains are still growing. Crying out loud, this is the time when you should be hitting nothing but live pitching."

"Yes!" Cruz whispered. He grinned and pointed at Tom.

"Later on," said Del Gato, "when you're older, the batting tee gets useful. But not yet. See, here's facts. From the time the pitcher throws the ball, the batter has only two tenths of a second to make three decisions. Where's it going—ball or strike? How fast is it going? And when do I start my swing so my bat will meet the ball at the perfect time and place? You can have the most beautiful swing in the world, but if you don't make these decisions in time, nothing else matters."

He turned and pointed. "María, your registration card says you pitch softball."

She blinked and gave him the tiniest nod Tom had ever seen.

"Warm up. I want you to throw some batting practice."

Now her head shook. "I can't. I only pitch underhand."

"*Cheese*, Louise! I know that. I want you to prove a point."

María took the mound and began her underhand warm-ups. Del Gato barked out a few commands, and she made some adjustments in her stride and release point to compensate for the new distance and height of the mound. Soon, she was throwing smooth, hard strikes. Tom loved watching her arm windmill over her head and the push of her legs. As she threw more pitches, her speed increased. So did the movement of the ball. It rose and dipped, not like a baseball pitch, but in ways Tom had never seen.

A few townspeople stopped scraping and sanding the old bleacher boards in the stands in order to watch the experiment. Even Doc, sitting up high in the shade, grinned and shook his head.

"This'll be fun," said Frankie, swinging a weighted bat, timing María's delivery, getting ready to be the first hitter. "Underhand pitches are so easy."

Wil stood with his mouth twisted into his cheek. "It's stupid," he muttered. "This won't help us. We're playing baseball, not softball."

Ramón shushed him. "A ball's a ball," he said. "What? You can't hit an underhand pitch?"

"I didn't say that. I'm just saying that if we don't want to get stomped on Saturday, we should start playing some real ball."

Cruz stepped close, swinging his maple bat, dusted with pine resin. "Listen to you, Wil," he said. "Come on. This is baseball! In baseball, all things are possible. Everyone knows that. Babe Ruth once hit a pop fly for a home run."

"He did not!" said Tara. "Is this another one of your dumb jokes?"

"I'm serious. It was on a real windy day, and he hit it so high, with so much spin, the ball blew back from left field to shortstop, and no one could catch it. He ran all the way to third base before it came down, then ran home when it took a big bounce."

"Wow!" said Cody. "That's what you call a Major League pop-up."

"Right. And on any given day, even the last-place team can beat any team in the league."

"But the Vikings are out of our league," said Clifford. "Wil saw them. He knows."

"They're good," said Wil. "Believe me. They're all-stars. And that pitcher they got, Sean Lemanski, throws a special pitch called a *murve*. That stands for 'murder curve.' And it *is*. It's really strange. Nobody can hit it."

Cruz held up his hands. "Guys, it's only Tuesday. A lot can happen between now and Saturday. Why don't we just bat against María, and humor this old man? Let's see how stupid this drill really is."

Turned out, the only thing stupid about the drill was how each boy felt after trying to pick up the flight of the ball and make solid contact with it. The underhand delivery, the spin, the trajectory—it was all so different.

Except for Cruz.

He had the benefit of being the last to bat, so watching the other boys and their mistakes must've helped.

But Tom soon realized it was more than that. Out of six

pitches, Cruz took six swings with his maple bat. And he hit the ball hard each time. No misses, no foul tips, no dribblers. Each one a solid line drive or deep fly.

It shouldn't have surprised Tom. Hadn't Cruz said that "on certain days" he could hit anything? Even so, Tom was beyond awe as he realized the full meaning of what he'd just seen. The other boys teased and joked that Cruz must've played a lot of girls' softball back home.

"Hey, Cruzie," yelled Clifford. "You play Bobby Sox? You're Miss *Natural* at this." And everyone laughed.

But Tom knew.

And so did Del Gato. At least he seemed to know. He did not react in a way anyone else would notice. But Tom noticed that during Cruz's entire at-bat, Del Gato squatted partway up the first-base line, studying everything Cruz did, watching his feet, his hands, his eyes.

Afterward, Del Gato gathered everyone together again. With his arms crossed over his chest, he spat out four words the team would begin to hear again and again. "Pathways in the brain," he said. "You see, I had you boys bat against María because I figured none of you'd ever seen an underhand fast-pitch before. Your brains are trained for a baseball delivery. But we have no pathways for the unfamiliar. So it baffles us. Now I don't care if we have four days left or four hours. It's never too late to begin forming new pathways. And the best way to do it is by repetition." Del Gato lifted his chin toward the mountain. "So get on back up that hill once more and work on making some new pathways. *Hee-yah!*"

If he'd had a whip, Tom was certain Del Gato would've cracked it.

The entire team dropped gloves and bats and scrambled across the dusty field, through the gate, and up the hill. This time, Rachel came down first, with Cruz and Clifford right behind. Once more, Tom finished last, but he had noticed something. The hill seemed smaller this time. And friendlier.

As practice resumed, the team worked on one basic drill after another. Soft-toss hitting drills, baserunning, bunting. They paired off and fielded a hundred ground balls in a row. Then took a hundred fly balls. Then they did it all over again.

Standing along the foul line in right field, Tom banged a fist into his glove and bent forward. From center field, Clifford hit sharp ground balls at him that Tom could follow until the last two feet. Then he'd shut his eyes, lift his chin, and stab at them with his glove.

"Keep your head down," Del Gato yelled. "See that ball into your mitt." He told Clifford, "Get closer and hit softer until he gets his timing."

About halfway through the second hundred grounders, Tom actually saw the ball enter his glove. Once. And for that one moment, he felt as if he'd discovered gold. No—better than that. A secret.

Finally, after a few hours, the new manager showed mercy. It was over. With the afternoon sun still two hands above the horizon, the tired, sore, worn-out ballplayers limped their way to the Greater-Ade jug and the patch of shade under a pepper tree.

"I'm gonna die," said María. She collapsed onto her back, stretching her arms out. "My legs ache, my shoulders ache, even my bones ache."

"Big deal," said Frankie, lying with his feet propped up on his equipment bag. "I'm so sore, my *hair* aches."

Cruz bopped Tom's arm. "Hey, Tomcat, bring on the murveball, huh? You saw what I did. Today was one of those days."

"One of what days?" called María.

Cruz spun around. "One of the best days of my life, Mary Flowers."

She sat up and gave him the crookedest grin. "What?"

He threw an arm around Ramón. "Today's the day I finally put two and two together—and get five."

Tara groaned. "You're bonkers, you know that?"

"Thank you. But as soon as I'm done eating, I'm going to grab my laptop, come back here, and have a little talk with Mr. Dante Del Gato."

"About what?" asked Clifford.

Cruz draped his other arm around Clifford. "The secret of hitting, *vato*. What else?"

"He said there was no secret, just hard work."

"Ah, but that's what everyone says when there really *is* a secret."

"Come and get it!" yelled Maggie LaRue. "*¡La cena! ¡Ándele!*" Someone rang a cowbell and the stampede was on. Sore bones or not, everyone was hungry. Tom pushed himself up off the grass and joined Clifford and Cruz heading to the smoky grills next to the grandstand.

The dinner buffet that night was the best so far. Maggie, Humberto, Daisy, and Mrs. Sabala had set out clay bowls of *mango y jalapeño* salsa, crumbled goat cheese, fresh *cilantro con limón*, lettuce, tomatoes, an iron skillet of Spanish rice with diced tomatoes and black olives, another with refried pinto and black beans smothered in cheese, three kilo baskets of warm tortillas under white cloth, and grilled chicken strips kept warm in a pan of bubbling brown sugar, tequila, ginger, and lime juice marinade.

"Fresh from the garden," said Maggie. "Eat up, *niños*!"

Cruz blew on a strip of *pollo asada* and stuck it in his mouth just to chew on while he loaded his plate. "Ah, chicken," he said, and swirled his fork in a wringing motion. "Hey, Tom. Breakfast of champions."

Tom winced at the memory.

Before they left the buffet table, two visitors arrived. And everyone noticed them right away.

Cruising up in a blue Cadillac with a white steerhead skull shellacked and bolted to the hood came the mayor, Oscar

Calabaza. Next to him, riding shotgun, sat the newest big landowner in town, the president and owner of First Nugget Mortgage and Loan, Alabaster Jones.

"What do you think they want?" said Mrs. Sabala.

Del Gato didn't hesitate. "They want this bunch to lose, that's what."

Hollis B ran up the bleacher boards, two at a time, to the score booth and jumped inside the open window.

Peering out from behind the worktable, he began to chant. "The mayor just arrived. The mayor himself. Just rode up, showed up, and chauffeured up old Mr. Jones, the money-man, who'll break your bones when you fall behind on a tractor loan. Ah, but everybody must get Jonesed." He clicked off his phone. "I gotta go!"

Hollis B crept backwards, toward the rear door of the booth, and disappeared just as the mayor made his way through the crowd, stepping right up to Tom's dad.

"How's it going, Coach Gallagher?" The mayor held up his chubby right hand, swung it behind him, then flung it forward, like pitching a horseshoe, to give Tom's dad a shake.

Mr. Gallagher shook. "Coming along fine, Oscar. Thank you."

"Good, good." He spun in a small circle. "Great to see everyone."

Most everyone looked away.

"Welcome to have dinner with us," said Tom's dad. "Both of you."

"Oh, no, no." He glanced quickly at Mr. Jones. "No, Al and

I just stopped by to extend our best wishes to the team. See how everyone's doing."

Alabaster Jones, dressed in white pants and a white sport coat, stared through tiny dark sunglasses while chewing gum at a hundred bites a minute.

Maggie slapped down her meat tongs and stepped forward. "We're doing just fine, Mayor *Gordo*, no thanks to you. We could use a couple portable potties out here. Since the town can't afford to keep the ballpark up, do you suppose it could afford to keep up an outhouse?"

"Of course, of course. There'll be one here tomorrow."

"We need two."

The mayor squinted hard, then broke into a smile. "Certainly. Of course. *Dos*." He held up two fingers, then shook them. "Peace."

"Bueno." Maggie picked up her tongs and returned to the grill. "Reason we need two," she went on to say, "is in case you come around again. Because they only hold so much."

Everyone laughed.

The mayor was a good sport about it, but Mr. Jones was not amused. He aimed his sunglasses at Mr. Gallagher, and in a voice like a rattlesnake rattling in spit, he said, "We understand you're getting some help. Some steroid-popping, double-crossing, drunken sleazeball kind of help."

Tom's mother rushed up and peered into his dark glasses. "Mr. Jones, how dare you slander Coach Del Gato. I'll have you know he's ten times the gentleman you are and a hundred times more important to this town."

The mayor interceded. "Helen, Helen, please. We're not

here to make a brouhaha. But as you know, the *gentleman* you refer to does have a reputation of sorts, and for him to be around all of these children, well—"

"Well, *what?*" Del Gato's voice boomed out of the grandstand. He strode up, past the table, past Tom, his laser glare fixed on the mayor. "You got a problem, Calabaza? Tell me to my face."

"Oh, no, you misunderstand," said the mayor. "I was about to say we've had phone calls about children screaming and running devil-may-care up and down the hillsides. And we are concerned."

Alabaster Jones pushed the mayor aside. "I got a problem." He stood face-to-face with Del Gato. "The kind of new residents we want to attract to this town are good, honest, high-classed people who are going to be very turned off by the likes of you. So do us all a favor and just crawl back into your truck and drive on out of here. Leave us civilized folk to work this matter out on our own."

"He'll do no such thing." Mr. Gallagher had worked his way alongside both men. "He's managing this team."

Del Gato raised an arm and gently moved Tom's dad back while he stared at the pink-faced man in the white suit. Tom saw Del Gato's jawline tremble, his hand clench into a hammer, then Del Gato stepped back. He turned and strode off, through the crowd, nearly knocking Tom over.

"Dante, wait." Tom's dad hustled after him.

No, he can't leave, thought Tom. He can't quit now!

Nearby, Cruz closed his eyes and dropped his head.

Tom's mother shook a fistful of plastic forks and knives at

the mayor. "Oscar! Jerry and I run this camp. We decide who comes and who goes and who coaches. And you two men have just worn out your welcome. Now, is there anything else? Because our dinner is waiting."

The mayor waved his hands, backing away. "No, no, please. We didn't mean to cause you any discomfort." He flashed his toothy smile into the crowd of stony faces. "Go, eat. Please. Enjoy yourselves."

"Yeah," said Mr. Jones, "the way Judas enjoyed the Last Supper."

The mayor bowed his head, crossed himself twice, and the two men left.

Later that night, Tom dumped a load of firewood into the pit. "What should we do?"

"Wait till tomorrow," said Cruz. "He'll be back."

"Well, we can still break out your CD-ROM tonight, right? So we can try it out?"

Cruz sat on the wooden bench, gripping his bat, taking short, quick swings at invisible pitches. His eyes peered into the distance. Tom could almost see the electrical processing going on inside his head. "Well, you can try it, Tom, but that's not the problem. Problem is, it's not quite ready yet. And it may be completely bogus, I don't know."

"What's bogus?" asked Cody, walking up. "What're you guys talking about?" The trio was tonight's fire makers, but Cody had showered first and arrived late.

"Same thing we always talk about," said Cruz as he stood and swung, blasting an imaginary ball over Cody's head.

"The secret of hitting." He hopped up onto the bench, peering off at another pitch. Then he slowly lowered his bat, but kept staring. "Hey, Tom. Oh, man!"

"Oh, man, what?" Tom hopped up next to him and followed his gaze. There, in the falling light, he saw Del Gato's old Chevy Apache pickup parked in Doc's driveway. "What's he doing up there?"

Cruz backhanded Tom in the ribs. "Who cares? Let me get my laptop and let's go." He turned. "Cody, more oak! We got the pine. But this fire'll need more hardwood. Might be up late tonight."

They stopped in the bunkhouse, then jogged across the Gallagher land, skirting the ball field, to the foot of Doc's drive. From there, Tom could see the two men sitting on the front porch, talking. He could only imagine what they were saying. "Maybe he's telling Doc to cancel the game. That he quit, and we stink, and it'll be a massacre."

Cruz didn't respond. Up the asphalt he strode, past the old pickup.

Tom ran behind. Near the orange trees, he cupped his hand to his mouth. "Hey, Doc!"

"Tom? That you?"

"Me and my friend Cruz."

"We were just talking about you boys. Come on up."

As they crossed through the ankle-high grass, Doc stood and walked to the porch rail. "So you're the boy from Paloma."

"Yes, sir. Cruz de la Cruz." He jogged the last few feet to the porch, extending his hand. "Pleased to meet you."

"Likewise, uh, *el gusto es mío*." Doc adjusted his glasses. "You boys care for some orange juice? Fresh squeezed. Just picked me a bunch."

"Sure."

"Sounds good," said Tom. "Thanks."

"Glad to." Doc turned toward the door, then paused. "Say, Tom, before I forget. Would you stop by early tomorrow morning, if you get a chance? Before camp?"

"Yeah, sure."

"Good."

As soon as Doc entered the house, Cruz leaned forward. Speaking softly, deliberately, he asked, "Mr. Del Gato, are you still going to coach our team?"

"You mean, am I going to quit?"

Cruz answered by widening his eyes.

Del Gato motioned for the boys to sit. Cruz pulled out a chair. Tom chose one farther away.

Del Gato peered out over clasped hands, holding his chin with his thumbs. His gaze drifted toward the Lucky Strike. "That field down there is where I grew up. Where my dogs ran for hours chasing balls during two-man batting practice with my brother. Those baselines down there hold my blood, sweat, spit. My tears. And the dirt and dust clouds are part of me."

He laid his arms flat on the table. "So, quit? *¡Chicharrones!*" He snorted, shaking his head. "Not a rat's chance. Only reason I left today was because I'm just not ready to go to jail over killing a guy for stupidity."

Cruz rapped his knuckles on the table. "All right!" He

looked at Tom, grinning. "Good. Then can I ask you something else?"

Del Gato lifted his palm. "Shoot."

"I got this idea that sounds crazy, but—" He waited a moment, then plunged. "I think it's possible to program yourself into being a perfect hitter. And I'd like to try it out on our team. See if I'm right."

Del Gato stared at Cruz. "That how you learned to hit so good?"

"Yeah."

"So, what's the trick?"

"I use a video game."

Del Gato cracked up, the first time Tom had ever heard him laugh.

Cruz was not deterred. "I'm serious. And I got the idea from you. From some old videos of you—of those last nineteen at-bats. I saw what you did each time you swung."

"A lot of people saw what I did."

"But I figured out a way for a guy to get those results every time."

Del Gato laughed again. "I don't see how." He lifted his chin at Cruz's computer. "Show me what you got."

Cruz hit the power button. While they all waited for the programs to load, Del Gato sat back, then closed his eyes. It was a long, slow blink that seemed to open again somewhere in the past. Above the soft clicks and musical tones of the laptop, he began to speak.

"Guys," he started, slowly, softly. "*Escúcheme.* Before you showed up tonight, Doc was talking to me about passing things on, about how it'd be a shame to go to my grave without passing something on."

Oh my gosh! thought Tom. The secret. Like in the prophecy. But does that mean he's going to die?

"So since you want to talk hitting, I'm thinking, why not? See, from the time I was two, my papa, my brother, my cousins—everyone—would pitch to me. Tennis balls, rubber balls, even rocks. And I'd swing at 'em. I'd use a broomstick, a bat, sometimes I even used Abuelita's cane. Didn't matter. Just loved to hit. Then, when I got older"—he looked up at the porch ceiling—"geez, I was about ten or eleven—I got so good, I'd pay any kid in town a buck for every strike he could slip past me. And I'd charge the guy a nickel for every hit I got. Some of those guys were three or four years older than me, too. But after a couple hundred pitches, we usually broke about even." He held up a finger. "The key was *repetición*."

He tapped his fingertips into his palm several times. "Hour after hour, this wind, that wind, I'd swing at pitches. I'd walk along trails and hit the flower tops off the yellow mustard plants. Come home, I'd swing at houseflies buzzing in the patio. Anything. I worked on changing the focus of my eyes at lightning speed. I did whatever I could think of to sharpen my reflexes and shorten my reaction time. Five, six, seven hours a day."

Cruz glanced at the screen. He clicked a few more keys.

Del Gato continued. "Nothing in that magic box of yours is going to match that. And by 1984, I got to where I could actually see the ball coming at me in slow motion. I mean, that's what it looked like. What I was really able to do was to speed up my brain processes to the point where I could, say, watch a bird flutter in midair and tell you the exact shape and color of its wings." He sipped his juice, then leaned back, folding his arms. "And that's when I conquered the art of hitting."

I can't believe I'm hearing this, thought Tom. That's what he did? It's true?

"And I saw him do it." Doc stood on the other side of the screen door, holding a tall glass in each hand. As Tom jumped up to get the door for him, Doc used his elbow to switch on the porch light. "Thank you, Thomas." He stepped down and placed the glasses on the chipped Formica tabletop. "Yes, sir, Dante here was pretty amazing in those days."

"The rest, guys, is history. Helped get the Padres to the play-offs. Then came the hitting streak, the '84 National League pennant." He paused. The silence lasted a long time.

Cruz lowered the bright green screen. The computer might've been ready to go, but the people weren't. Cruz whispered his next question. "But then what happened? Why'd you quit?"

Del Gato got up and stood with his back to them, gazing into the valley. "I made a choice. I thought it was right. Something just told me that this sport was one thing we ought to preserve. As is. Especially the World Series. To me, that's sacred ground." He shrugged a shoulder. "I don't know, I just felt that if I kept playing, I'd start to feel worse and worse about what I was doing. It'd be like if you were a poker player who could see everyone's cards. Sure, you'd always win, get as rich as you want, all kinds of fame and glory. But I'd always played ball with integrity. For the love of the game. And so, as it turned out, that was also the reason I quit."

Whoa, thought Tom. There it is. A deep, dark secret. But not the one I expected.

Del Gato turned around, grinned slightly, and glanced at Doc. A flush of embarrassment seemed to rise up. He reached down, grabbed his glass, and finished off his juice. "Doc? Nice to see you again. Thanks for the O.J."

"Not at all. And listen—don't be a stranger."

Del Gato looked at Cruz. "I still want to see that thing." Then he turned and left. They watched him cross the lawn to the driveway, creak open the dented door of his truck, and climb inside. No one spoke until the single red taillight on the old Chevy disappeared down the hill.

"He doesn't like good-byes," said Doc.

Cruz lifted his glass. "Neither do I."

When Cruz and Tom returned to camp, Cody waved at them from the fire ring with a triple-marshmallow torch. Frankie, Rachel, and Tara sat rocking sideways on the block wall along the deck, joining Mr. Gallagher and his guitar in singing old sitcom themes and the folk songs Tom had grown up hearing. His dad loved that old music.

Most of the other players seemed intent on building triple-decker s'mores. And as he and Cruz walked past, Tom kept thinking, just as intently, about what Del Gato had revealed.

Cruz tore off his shirt.

"The way I see it," he said, "we've got three days to reprogram the neural responses in nine brains so that by Saturday they can read the baseball out of Sean Lemanski's hand as easy as they read a book."

"Three days," Tom muttered, "to conquer hitting. But how? After what we heard tonight."

They entered the bunkhouse. "Well, I don't know about you," said Cruz, "but I'm going to take a long, hot shower and try to figure that out." He kicked off his shoes and unbuttoned his jeans.

"Save me some hot water," said Tom. He wanted to sketch out a few ideas while alone. "I'll take mine after you're done."

"And I'll yell stuff," Cruz yelled from the shower room. "*Número uno.* Tom, how many computers does your mom have in the library?"

"Five."

"Perfect. *Cinco y cinco.* We can work in shifts. Okay, any chance they've got 3-D accelerator cards inside?"

"Yep."

"*Compadre*, this is too easy. Okay, now my little problem. And for that, you need to break out your notebook."

Tom walked into the shower room and talked directly to the curtain. "How do you know about my notebook?"

"Everybody knows about it. María wants to steal it and see what you think about her."

"She does? When did she tell you that?"

"Today at lunchtime, when you went off to write."

"*What?* They knew I was writing?"

"Well, sure." He looked out from behind the curtain. "That's why we left you alone. I thought you knew that."

"I don't know anything. Except you're getting water everywhere. So what else did she say?"

Cruz disappeared. "Nothing, that was it. But I think she likes you."

"What do you mean? She thinks I'm some dumb, clumsy dorko-doofus."

"No way, not at all, *vato.* She doesn't think you're clumsy. And she was smiling."

Tom broke open his Dreamsketcher. "Okay, okay, forget it. Let's get to your problem. Talking about María makes me nervous."

"*¡Está bien!* Okay, we need to figure out how to get the computer to read the swing."

"What do you mean?"

"Well, the screen shows a pitcher throwing a ball. You stand there and swing just as the ball leaves the screen. And the computer knows exactly where the ball is at all times—even in the ether—but I don't know how to get the computer to determine the bat's location—the arc and speed of the swing. I've tried a bunch of stuff."

Cruz shut off the water, and the room went still. "You have to know that to know if you're making solid contact. I was hoping Del Gato could help us or tell us if we even need it, once he got a look at the game." He grabbed a towel off the metal hook.

In his notebook, Tom drew a top-down view of a stick-man batter standing in front of a monitor. "Hey," he said. "How did *you* do it? How did you get so good?"

"Well, I only got this design to where it is last week. For the past year or so, I've just been using it like batting practice. I just stand there and swing. It really does help your eyes."

Tom closed his notebook. "Okay, why don't we just do that?"

"Because now the program's so close to being perfect. And Tom, we only have three days. Not three years."

Under the stars that night, just about the whole team was huddled around Ramón's telescope, perched on its tripod, aimed at the planet Saturn.

"Those rings," said Rachel. "I never knew they looked like

that! They're like these beautiful silver highways circling a giant pearl."

"They're just a bunch of dust and rocks and boulders," said Frankie.

So are the hills around us, thought Tom as he stood outside the group, following a slow-moving satellite as it inched across the sky. And from up there, he knew, the earth and all its rocks looked like a big, beautiful gemstone, too.

"Yeah, maybe it's only space dust," said Ramón, "but the thing is, what really exists out there is so much more than we can imagine. At least, it has been so far. Once, the Hubble telescope sent back pictures of two galaxies colliding at full force, ten million light-years away, spitting out stars and pieces of stars like they were exploding from this monstrous galactic train wreck. Stuff like that goes on all the time out there. Who could've imagined that?"

"I could've," said Tom in a quiet voice. Then he felt the attention. "I mean, I think we all could've if we had the chance. But imagining takes time. And it's hard to get around to thinking about everything."

For a moment, silence filled the campsite. *Imagining takes time.*

Then Cruz appeared from out of the bunkhouse, striding up. "Listen, you guys. I have to show you something." He opened his computer and a bright green baseball field glowed from the screen. "See this? I have a CD here that holds one of the greatest secrets of the universe. The secret of hitting."

"Oh, what?" said María, pulling her long hair back and

slipping on an elastic band. "Some dumb video game? Now that's imagination!"

"No, no, look. This is how I learned to hit so good." He pulled up a lawn chair and set the laptop on it.

Wil grunted. "Well, that's great, if María's pitching, and we're playing girls' softball."

"Eat cactus and die, Wil," María blurted. "I made you look sick."

"You guys," said Cruz. "Really. I think this thing would even work for tennis. Look, they use video simulators in the Air Force to teach pilots how to fly jets, right?"

"Yeah, " said Clifford. "My brother's in the Air Force."

"Okay. And you've seen race-car simulators and snowboard simulators and everything, like at the arcade, right?"

"Sure," María agreed, "but they're so phony."

"All right, but still, I figured, why couldn't I dream up a video simulation so realistic that it could teach me how to be a great hitter?"

Ramón knelt closer for a better look. "What's it do?"

"What happens is," said Cruz, "you see the same pitch, pitch after pitch, by the hundreds. So right away, you get tons better at tracking the ball, because it's so realistic. Your focus becomes extreme. Pretty soon, you're picking up the spin of the ball, you're reading the arc, your brain gets quicker at analyzing speed and location."

"But no pitcher pitches the same way each time," said María.

Cruz agreed. "That's why we can program in four or five release points and maybe two or three different arm angles for the same pitch—say, for example, a murveball." He grinned.

"Plus, we can vary the speed. Pretty soon, you won't just be guessing where the ball will be, you'll actually calculate its path ahead of time and then meet it there with your bat."

"Oh," said Rachel. She paused a moment. "So, it's like running down a mountain. You see the path way out ahead, so you know right where you'll put your feet without stopping to think about it."

Cruz nodded. "Yeah. Only we do it with a bat and ball." And everyone seemed to be imagining that.

"Start it," said Wil. "Let's see how it works."

Cruz waved his arm. "Ladies and gentlemen," he said. "I introduce to you the HitSim. Brought to you by Cruz-on.com."

"The HitSim?" said Tom.

"That's right. The hitting simulation game that turns anyone into a superstar who 'HitSim where they ain't.' "

Cruz not only ran the disk, showing all the variables and settings, but he paralleled his secret method to Del Gato's method, which, he pointed out, was so perfect, the guy had to quit baseball. By the end of his little show, all of the players were sitting up on their bags, barely able to speak.

"What Tom and I found out," he went on, "was that Del Gato's method works best if you start real young and work like crazy. Very few people could copy what he did. But once we perfect this baby . . ." He let the words hang there, above his grin, like a soft curve.

"And if we start right away, by Friday we could see and hit hundreds and hundreds of pitches. We'll see murveballs flying at us in our sleep. By Saturday, man, that Lemanski's not going to fool *any*one. I'm serious."

Rachel and Tara turned to each other. Tom caught María's glance. She widened her eyes, then gave him a smile. He quickly looked away.

Ramón lay back down. "So that's why Del Gato quit? He discovered something that gave him an unfair advantage?"

Cruz nodded. "That's what he told us."

María hugged her knees and rocked back. "Wow," she said. "Now I see the guy all different."

"Yeah," Wil added. "Me, too. Could you imagine some guy today quitting because of that? Because he was too good?"

Cruz started another simulation using a different pitcher. "I don't know," he said. "But I'd like to think there might be one or two."

After a few moments, Ramón asked, "So, you wrote this program?"

"I didn't even have to. I adapted it from a video simulator program called Yer.in.There by PaladinWire."

"Really?" said Tom. "I have that. What version?"

"Eight."

"Eight?" Ramón sounded suspicious. "It only came out in version six last month."

"Oh, yeah. I know." Cruz paused a moment, tapping a few keys and folding the screen back out of view. "Yeah, well, this one's experimental. I know a guy who knows a guy who works for Paladin."

"You are so lucky," said Frankie.

Now Clifford had doubts. "But there's one thing I don't get. How do you know if you really hit the ball?"

Cruz had no ready answer for that one. He shrugged. "Haven't quite worked that out yet."

That news seemed to shift the mood. It was as if rain had just begun to fall at the start of a ball game. Tom lay back down, feeling exhausted.

"Still," said Frankie. "It's got to do us some good. I mean, it's pretty amazing. And it sure helped you." His voice was upbeat, but this time Frankie's optimistic spirit was not contagious.

Tom stared at the sky, watching an airplane fly over. His eyes drifted until he spotted the small starglow of another satellite. A thought blew in. Suddenly he bolted straight up.

"That's it!" he whispered. "I think I got it." He stood on his bag, in T-shirt and shorts, pacing to one end, then back again. "Oh, wow. Cruz, maybe you were looking at it all wrong." He pointed to the center of the sky. "Maybe you should've been looking at it from up there."

"Up there? What for?"

Tom looked at Cruz and he could not stop a smile. "You know those Global Positioning satellites that pick up radio signals so they can track the location of a stolen car or something? What if we got some minicams and set up something like that?"

"What do you mean? How would it work?"

"Well, like a GPS network, sort of. But instead of sending radio waves from a car to the satellites, we'll send video images of the bat to the computer. We just have to turn the bat's sweet spot into somebody's stolen car—and pinpoint its location using video cameras!"

Now it was Cruz who couldn't stop a smile.

On Wednesday morning, Tom woke early and with an urgency. He wanted to write down as much as he could about what had happened last night. From murveballs to stolen cars. He even jotted down a few things to ask Doc, though the questions caused his stomach to swirl.

By the time the sun had broken through the trees, Tom had tended the horses, grabbed Doc's newspaper, yanked out the sports section, and plunked himself down in a chair on Doc's front porch. But he hadn't even had a chance to swallow his first gulp of orange juice before Doc threw him a murveball of his own.

"Tom," he said. "Will you forgive me?"

Slowly, Tom flattened the newspaper without looking up. "For what?"

"For putting this burden on you. My gosh, what was I thinking?"

Tom sat back and studied the shreds of white pulp floating in his blue plastic cup. "It's okay, Doc. We're going to be all right."

"Not if you lose, you won't."

Tom nodded. "Yeah, that's true."

Doc stared off toward the ball field. "The past few days have been like old times around here. I've seen the folks come out, making music, barbecuing, carrying on. Seen you kids down there laughing and yelling, working your hearts out. Then last night, Mr. Del Gato asked me outright, would I miss all that whooping and hollering riding up from the ball field, would I miss the smoke of that taco meat frying on the grill?" He looked at Tom. "Imagine him being that sentimental."

Tom squeezed his lips tight and imagined.

"Well, he is. Sometimes, sometimes not. He has good days and bad, like the rest of us. He's fought a mountain of sadness over the years. But last night, he never condemned me for what I'd done, never said a cross word. Just pointed out the fact that people are coming here to the ballpark in the middle of the week, poor people who are chipping in for food, bringing tools, working on the field. Some of them old boys are going to start painting the bleachers this morning to get ready for Saturday's crowd."

Doc pushed his juice glass away, folded his hands together, and looked Tom straight in the eye. He spoke slowly. "Here's what I learned in the last two days, Tom. We live a life out here that only poor, simple folks can enjoy. Rich people can't afford to live like us. They don't have the time."

Tom did not respond, but he figured he knew what Doc meant.

"And now I put it all on the line." Doc closed his eyes. "What was I thinking? Tom, I'm sorry. I'm a man of my word and I'll stick by it—but I'll be pulling for you."

"It's okay, Doc." Tom fumbled for his notebook, trying to slip the black band off, hoping to find a question inside or something. He glanced down and saw two words. *El campo.*

"Doc, what about that Indian site up there? What if they can't build on that land? What if it's sacred?"

Doc looked at him as if he'd just woken from a dream. "Indian site? Oh, yeah, they know all about that. Developers took care of that last year. It's all been looked at and recorded. They say it's not important enough. Won't stop the project."

That was bad news. Tom hummed a grunt, then glanced back down at his book.

"You still taking notes on life, are you, Tom? That's something I wish I did, your age. I bet you'll end up with one whiz-bang story after this whole mess is over and done with, don't you think?"

Tom slowly hid the notebook under his hands. "I guess so."

"Would you mind if I wrote something in your book? I'd consider it quite an honor if I could."

"Well, I don't know." Tom grinned in embarrassment. "I guess. Sure, it'd be an honor to have you do it."

"Nothing special," said Doc. "Just another little note of encouragement." He took the book and smoothed down the very last page, then brought out his pen. "Back page is perfect. When you get there, then maybe the words of an old man might give you a lift. Or make you laugh."

"Both, I bet," said Tom, pushing back his chair. Now he felt like doing something for Doc. "I'm going to pick you some more oranges."

"Good. Get the high up ones, will you? Can't reach 'em anymore."

Before long, Tom had picked a shirtful. He trudged back up to the porch just as Doc was recapping the pen.

"Thank you, Thomas. Just set them there in that box."

Tom knelt near a stack of small, wooden citrus crates and spilled the contents of his shirt into one.

"Tom!" someone yelled. "Tom!" It was Cody, running up the drive. "We're starting! Come on! There's a TV crew here! Hurry up. We're starting practice in the *barn*."

"What?" A TV crew? he thought. Why would they be here?

"Okay, okay, I'll be right down." He turned to Doc, realizing he needed to say something to let Doc know that of course he had forgiven him, that it wasn't even a matter of forgiveness.

As Tom reached around for the right words, Doc smiled up at him. "Tell me, Tom. Think you'll end up writing books? I mean, for a living?"

Tom hunched his shoulders. He had considered it. "Some guys do."

Doc stood and held out the Dreamsketcher. "Son, you will, too, one day. You're on the right track here. Mark my words. One of these days this book here'll be worth a lot of money."

Tom grinned at that. "Thanks, Doc." Then a wild thought hit him like a knockdown pitch. Had Doc leafed through the pages? Had he seen his dreamsketches? Had he read his "what if"s about María and Cruz and what he *wished* he would've said to Doc?

Tom reached for the book with a shaky hand. "But, um,

I don't think I should count on it. My dad says you got a better chance of hitting the lottery or a Pedro Martinez fastball than making money writing books."

Doc held on a bit longer. "Well, maybe so, but every week somebody hits the lottery. And somebody hits Pedro. Why not you?" He let go.

Cutting through Doc's pasture above the ball field, Tom saw a white van with a TV satellite dish on top parked behind the outfield wall. As he crossed the road toward home, he heard a generator inside the van roar to life. Two men— one a sports reporter Tom recognized from a local TV station—stood at the rear doors, gathering equipment and laying out thick black cable.

Cody and Frankie met Tom as he ran up to his yard. "Why are those TV guys here?"

"Because of the game," said Frankie. "There's a story in the paper this morning about Del Gato."

"There is? What'd it say?"

"Headlines were 'Del Gato Lays It on the Line for Dillontown Nine.' It was so cool."

"You serious?"

"Come on," said Cody. "Del Gato wants us in the barn."

Tom began taking rapid steps. "Why the barn?"

Frankie slung an arm around him and pointed. "See that blue SUV? That's another reporter and a photographer. This place is like me, *vato*. It's getting kind of popular. And Del Gato's getting kind of nervous."

Inside the barn, Mrs. Gallagher stood in the center of a group sprawled out on hay bales, oil drums, and scattered avocado crates. María and Clifford stood holding a string of Christmas lights that ran between them from one side to the other.

"I was hoping," said Mrs. Gallagher, "that this would not happen. Jerry and I had hoped that the media would leave us alone."

"Are we going to be famous?" asked Wil, thrusting out a flexed arm.

Tara stood and flicked back her dark brown hair. "I need to get an agent. I need a stylist."

"You need to be yourselves, all of you. But in this country, we have a free press, which we cherish. So we'll have to do the best we can while these reporters go about their business."

"They won't bother us," Del Gato growled from a dusty wooden hay cart. "I'll give 'em hell's bells, the bunch of 'em. If they want an interview, tell 'em to come see me first. And I'll rip 'em a new throat."

Tom almost grinned. Suddenly, after all he now knew, he was beginning to see Del Gato's crabby shell as nothing more than armor.

Tom's dad coughed softly. "Yes, well, the important thing is that we stay focused." He strode to the center of the barn. "And in that regard, Mr. Del Gato has set up a focus drill using this string of lights."

"Plug 'em in!" said Del Gato.

Frankie shoved an orange extension cord into a bare outlet near the barn door. The colored lights lit up one at a time, in a rolling sequence, as if running back and forth between one side of the barn and the other.

"My dad," said Del Gato, "used to set me up with fifty feet

of Christmas lights just like these. And I'd stand like this." He walked to María, took the end of the string, and held it to his face.

"The line would run between my nose and a fence post, but the drill can be done from any angle. You want to get to the point where you can follow each light down the line and back, focusing on every single color, one bulb at a time, as fast as they go. Right now, it's about twenty miles an hour. A lot slower than a baseball."

Silence in the barn.

"Eventually, we'll speed it up."

Every eye seemed fixed on the moving lights, which appeared to be traveling like sixty to Tom. Red, blue, blur, blur, green, white, blur.

"Now, after lunch, I understand, all of you want to go to the library and try Cruz's deal, that video game." He glanced up. "That right, Cruz?"

"Yes."

Del Gato nodded. "Okay. We'll start with this drill, building your eyes and better focus skills. Then, we'll go to the field and do our regular workouts. Then at four o'clock, we'll hit the library."

After nearly a half hour of spotting light flashes with one eye, two eyes, near and far, Tom and a team of blinking, rapid-eyed ballplayers followed Del Gato from the barn to the edge of the ball field.

Tom, relieved to be outside, now noticed two TV news vans on site along with the car from the *San Diego Union-*

Tribune. The reporters ran up with camera crews, jostling alongside the team, calling out questions.

"Mr. Del Gato, why did you decide to come back and help the team?"

"Does this town still mean a lot to you?" asked another.

Walking backwards, one woman thrust out her mike. "Is this Big Game any replacement for the World Series games you missed? And does this mean you're back?"

As he had for years, Del Gato ignored them as if they were just a bunch of hecklers in the cheap seats. Lots of local fans gave interviews, though. Daisy Ramirez gave the historical perspective. Hollis B talked on the phone while the cameras rolled and talked even more when they stopped. Tom caught part of it as he walked by.

"No, I ain't homeless," Hollis B barked into his phone. "I'm a tramp. Anyone can be without a home, out on your own, like a rolling bone, but it takes pluck and spunk to ride *el mundo* in the breeze of the trees like *un vagabundo*!"

The woman TV news reporter ventured forth. "You seem to have a unique perspective on housing. How do you feel about this proposal?"

"Suppose you were an idiot," Hollis B started. "And suppose you were the mayor of Dillontown. Ah, but I repeat myself." He snapped his phone shut. "I gotta go."

Throughout the morning, more and more people appeared. Outsiders, insiders. The band. The mayor. The sheriff. Alabaster Jones.

By noon, a local radio talk show called "The Bullit Train" with host "Dodge" Bullit had set up shop in the score booth and placed extra loudspeakers on both wings of the stands so everyone could hear.

"Two hot topics up for discussion today," said Dodge Bullit as he began the show in front of a live lunchtime audience of Wildcats and their fans. Tom sat between Frankie and Cruz, who each straddled the bleacher board so they could see the show.

"One is the return of Dante Del Gato to public view after nearly twenty years of living in relative seclusion. The other topic is the surreal situation of having a baseball game decide the fate of a town. And today, I have with me the mayor of Dillontown, Oscar Calabaza, who is in favor of the new housing project." Scattered applause and boos and a lot of laughter greeted the mayor, who waved wildly, knocking over his microphone.

"Also joining us is a local businesswoman, Ms. Maggie LaRue, who opposes the development." Maggie popped up, threw both arms in the air and shook them. That triggered loud cheers. In the front row, Jimbo Jakes pounded his tom-tom, his skinny arms becoming blurs.

"Ms. LaRue, let me start by asking about your comment in today's paper that 'urban sprawl has turned into country crawl.' "

"It has. I own a hair salon here in town. I don't make much money, but I choose to live where I work. But these outsiders pushing for this thing, and the people buying their fancy homes, they want to live in the country and work in town. What kind of *idioto* wants to spend two hours a day in traffic?"

"Well, you just described about half the people in this county."

"That's what I'm saying. That's the difference. They don't want to stop and smell any roses. We do. And we don't just stop and smell these roses. We stop and *grow* these roses."

"Mr. Mayor, how do you respond?"

"Well, Dodge—if I may call you Dodge—for many years we town leaders have placed various proposals before the County Planning Board and people such as Ms. LaRue—"

"Maggie! My name is Maggie, you blimphead."

"Ah-hum. *People* have had plenty of time to raise objections. This project is consistent with the Dillontown Community Plan."

"Sure, Oscar, since you and your buddies wrote that, too."

"Even so, we have a site plan approved by the County. We have preliminary approval from the Building Department, positive environmental reports, and support all along by the key landowners. Until, of course, last Sunday night."

"Ah, yes," said Mr. Bullit. " 'Doc's Shock,' as it's being called. We've read about that. How could the project promoters let it come down to this, a youth baseball game? Why didn't they lock up the land rights first?"

"They thought they had. Around here, a man's word is sacred. And they felt Doc had given his word. But, as you know, this is also rugged country, and people out here tend to be rugged individuals, so—"

"So," Dodge interrupted, "one key landowner, Dr. Ken Altenheimer, decided to give Dillontown its own little World Series. A life-or-death match of dramatic proportions."

"Ah, no, it's just a friendly baseball game." The mayor smiled and waved again, now noticing a few TV cameras pointed his way. "Of course, I'd like to see the project go forward immediately, but Doc is an old friend, and we will certainly honor his wishes to let the ball game decide."

Maggie tossed both hands in the air. "You don't have a choice! Doc did *not* commit to you people." She drummed the back of one hand into the palm of the other. "You just thought you could pressure an old man."

"That right, Mayor?"

Again the mayor smiled. "No, no, we put no pressure on him. This deal is very good for the town, and we just made sure Doc understood."

"Let's take a call from our listeners," said Mr. Bullit. "Hello, Alfonso, you're on the Bullit Train!"

"Thanks. I live in Dillontown and I work in San Diego and I want to say that we always used to have holiday celebrations, Fourth of July, *Cinco de Mayo*, all that, and it was a real community thing. But those events take a lot of time and organization, and these days people're too busy. Not everyone can run a local business like Maggie. So if we're spending two hours a day in traffic, why *not* give us a better road so we can get home sooner? Then maybe we'd have more time for community events."

"Hey, Alfonso," said Maggie, "I got a better idea. Why not live where you work or work where you live? Instead, you pollute the air, then ask everyone else to solve your problems."

The mayor answered for him. "Simple solutions are for

simple minds, Maggie. I learned that in kindergarten. Besides, our plan brings jobs to the community and a community park. With no complications."

Mr. Bullit waved his hand. "Thanks for the call, Alfonso. Now I'd really like to hear from a ballplayer." He scanned the crowd, settling his eyes on Tom. "What about you down there?"

No! No! thought Tom. He shuddered and dropped his head almost into his *chile adovada*.

"Sure," said Cruz. He rose, bouncing toward the booth. Tom turtle-necked a peek, amazed that Cruz would volunteer to speak on the radio. He didn't enter the booth, though. He merely leaned in through the window.

"Thank you, young man," said Mr. Bullit. "So tell me, as a ballplayer, how do you feel about the plan to bury the ballpark?"

"Makes me feel just like my great-great-grandparents did when the settlers came in and moved them off their native lands. Because that's what these people want to do."

The mayor slammed the tabletop. "No one wants to move anyone off any land. That's laughable. They only want to build beautiful homes in beautiful country."

Cruz did not back down. "Well, sure, you're right. And I know you mean well, but in order to do that, they'll have to scrape the hills, fill in the canyons, build new roads, put in sidewalks, fences, curbs, and gutters. Before they're done, they will bury this land." He turned and looked at everyone. "Think about it. Lots of Americans go all day and never once touch the earth. They walk from carpet to tile to pavement to concrete, they sit in their cars and drive and drive, and never once set foot on the earth. And when you're off the earth, you're off the land. And that's why I say what they want to do is move us off the land."

The crowd exploded in applause and whistles. Tom had never heard anything so elegant, or eloquent, or whatever the word was to describe a guy's speech that pretty much summed up everything that was in his gut in just a few words.

That's because he travels, thought Tom. He's out there under the stars or cruising back roads and mesas, and you get time to think about stuff like that when you can just let your thoughts fly off as far as they can go.

Maybe, just maybe, Tom could write words as good as that. But he could never talk them. And on the radio, in front of a big ol' crowd like this? Never in a million years.

After lunch, the players resumed practice, working all afternoon on their game positions—the ones Del Gato thought would help the team most.

Cruz would pitch. Wil, catch. María, being so tall, would play first base, with Tara at second. Frankie, of course, was shortstop, and Clifford, third base. The outfield would be Ramón in left, Rachel in center, with Cody and Tom taking turns in right.

Cruz began warming up to throw another quick round of batting practice. Tom enjoyed batting against Cruz. Every pitch was over the middle and easy to follow. Except when he threw his sinker-curve. "My cross-fire hurricane pitch," he called it.

And it was. Instead of throwing overhand or three-quarter arm, on this pitch he'd drop down sidearm and fire a ball that cut across the plate at a vicious angle, then sank.

No one complained. It was good practice for Cruz to get ready for Saturday, and a challenge for the batter to follow the ball. But Tom had a hard enough time hitting normal pitches. He practically gave up when he saw the big sidearm sinker-curve heading his way.

As Cruz loosened up, Tom and Frankie stood alongside watching.

"Here's how I hold it," said Cruz. "You try it. For fun."

Tom held the ball while Cruz demonstrated the grip. "Put your middle finger on top of your pointing finger so it makes an X. Then when you throw it, come down sidearm." He demonstrated. "Fire it across your body, and it'll spin like a hurricane. And if the wind's just right, whoa, it's hard to hit. That's why I call it my cross-fire hurricane."

Cruz showed him once more. It felt funny to Tom, as if he didn't have a real grip on the ball. But when he threw it, the ball did seem to break. Not as much as Cruz's. Still, it cut across the plate and down. "Hey!" said Tom. "That's fun. That's my first curveball ever."

"Really? Because you got pretty good form."

"I do?" Tom exchanged laughs with Frankie, who was the only one who knew that if Tom had any baseball skill at all, it was in his arm. Not the strength of it—he was too slow to pitch—but his accuracy. One result, Tom figured, of throwing so many pitches to Frankie when they were younger.

He threw a few more for Cruz.

"Better," he said. "Keep trying. Takes a while to get the feel. But I do like your form." He bent down and scooped up a handful of dirt. He tossed the dry clay straight up.

"Why'd you do that?" asked Frankie.

"Because the trouble with this pitch is, I never know until game time whether or not I have it. All depends on the wind. So I always check." The dust drifted sideways, toward the east. "See that? Blowing just right. A little crosswind. That's all it needs."

Cruz resumed warming up. "Next time, Tom, just push off a little stronger with your right leg and take a longer step with your left. See how that works. And remember, you're launching a hurricane."

Next time? Tom wondered. Did Cruz actually think there'd be a next time? Before he could ask, Del Gato yelled, "Hey! Take your spots! Don't have all day." He spun toward the dugout. "Rachel, first batter."

Tom ran to the outfield. And he noticed he was running smoother—and with better form—than ever before. He felt stronger, bolder.

Like he could launch a hurricane.

Mountain winds can be tricky. The same gentle breeze that blows inland off the Pacific Ocean can roar as it rides up the mountainsides past Dillontown. Warm and humid air forms cumulonimbus thunderclouds that tower in the summer afternoons, stacked high above the 5,500-foot-high mountain range, but stalled right there by the arid eastern winds roiling up from the desert floor.

So thunderstorms form, bringing three or four inches of rain in one day to the lush western slopes, while just over the top of the ridge, the desert scape is lucky to get four inches of rainfall in a year.

Then there are days when the east wind wins. Hot, dry gusts cross the barren sands, climb the red granite ridges, and blow all the way down to the sea, drying out eyes, houseplants, and sagebrush terrain along the way.

A lot depends upon the wind.

Around four o'clock Wednesday afternoon, the players gathered at the Gallagher farm. Each one grabbed two baseball bats and jogged to the school library, about half a mile away. Mrs. Gallagher had already pushed the tables against the walls and set up five "batting stations," complete with paper home plates, around the room.

"You know, Cruz, you might just have something here,"

Mr. Gallagher observed. "Did you know there's clear scientific evidence that the neural pathways in our brains can be altered by repetitious action?"

"Yes, I've heard that." Cruz gave him a serious look. "But you know, I had to hear it over and over about a hundred times before it sank in."

"Tom," said his mother. "I've got five more minicams. That makes ten total with the school's collection. Everything else you asked for is in that orange bag." She pointed to a table near the door. "A big roll of red Velcro, scissors, and tape."

"Velcro?" said Frankie. "What for?"

"Well, here's what I was thinking. First, we strap a piece of Velcro around the sweet spot of each bat. Then we set up a camera above each station, pointing down at home plate. That lets us view the front-to-back motion of everyone's swing. Then, if we set up another camera behind each batter, we can videotape the height of the swing."

"Okay, wait," said Ramón, scribbling circles and lines on the white board. "The cameras record the two planes of the bat, and we combine that information to get the bat's location. And since the computer knows exactly where the ball is, the computer puts it all together and tells us where the bat contacts the ball. Right?"

Every head in the room, including Del Gato's, turned toward Tom. "Well, yeah," he said. "That's the basic idea."

Cruz eyed the white board. "But how do the cameras gather the information? And how does that info get to the computer?"

"Oh," said Tom. "Like this." He cut a strip of Velcro and stuck it to the bat, about three inches from the end of the barrel.

"Okay, now we just program the computer to disregard all video input from the cameras except for the color red." He looked around. "So no red batting gloves. Anyway, after that, the software plots the bat and the ball on a 3-D matrix inside the computer, and *abracadabra*, we have the best virtual batting practice ever invented."

For several heartbeats, Tom stood stunned. It was not so much for having been able to explain his ideas to everyone, but that *abracadabra*—he had never said anything as flashy as that before.

"Whoa," said Wil. Ramón and Cruz were scratching and nodding. Everyone else was buzzing and pointing.

"That's amazing," said María. "I love it!"

Clifford and Cody began installing the minicameras, two to a station, taping one to the ceiling and one to the back of a chair. Tara cut up the Velcro and began attaching it to all of the bats, lightweight and heavy, so the batters could choose the appropriate weapons in each case.

"Anybody know what a murveball looks like?" Cruz asked from his computer desk. "What it does? How fast it goes?"

"Yeah," said Wil. "I saw plenty of them in the Easter tournament."

"Cool, come over here and describe it. How does it look when you're standing up to bat?"

"I don't know."

"What?"

"Lemanski was on my team."

Everyone groaned. Cruz paused a moment. "Okay, okay," he said, "so were you catching? That's even better."

Wil shook his head. "No, sorry. First base."

Cruz spun around in his seat and looked at Wil. "Doesn't help. We need the batter's perspective." He addressed his crew. "Look guys, we need to know his release point, the arc of the ball, the spin, the speed, everything."

"Wait," said Wil. "My dad's got video. Would that help?"

"Help?" Cruz slumped in the chair, staring at the keyboard. "Yes, Wil. That would help. Could you possibly go get it?"

Wil darted out the door.

They worked into dinnertime, which didn't deter Maggie and the gang from serving *la cena*. "Three dozen *tacos al pastor!*" she said, breezing through the doorway with a cardboard box on her shoulder, crimped up against her red-, white-, and blue-tipped hair.

Everyone ate at their stations, whether they were testing for "red data only" readings or tweaking the program to be able to do it.

Finally, around seven o'clock, everything seemed to be in place and "close enough for horseshoes," according to Del Gato. So he gave the command for a full-blown test.

"Set your gizmo up right here," he said. "See what you've got so far."

Cruz seemed happy to oblige. With Wil's video, he could duplicate Lemanski's murve and his delivery, adjusted to the batter's point of view. He typed a few more entries.

The screen lit green, showing a virtual pitcher standing

on a video mound in the middle of a grassy field. "Here's
Lemanski, right-hander, five foot eight. On the screen he's
the exact size he'd be if you were standing at the plate looking out at him on the mound."

The pitcher wound up. "This is fifty-five miles an hour,"
said Cruz. A baseball left the pitcher's hand and sped toward
home plate, looking as if it would pop right out of the screen.

"Whoa!" everyone yelled.

"That looks so real!" said Tara. "That's bigger and better
than what you showed us last night."

Cruz rolled his chair backwards and grabbed his maplewood from against a bookcase. He stood. "Okay, guys, give
me room."

They gave him room.

He turned sideways, as if stepping into a batter's box, and
glared at the nineteen-inch monitor perched on a stack of
books. "All right, Ramón. Hit ENTER."

He did, the pitcher pitched, and Cruz swung.

The video ball flew over the wall.

Frankie whooped. "Oh, man, that's incredible! I want to
try it!"

"Wait," said Cruz. "Look."

Immediately the screen filled with a table of stats.

RESULT	DISTANCE	CONTACT
Home run	285 feet	Solid

Twelve seconds later, he did it again. And then again.

Home run. Home run. Home run.

The library exploded with dancing and cheers.

19

Thursday morning, bright and early, everyone woke to the sound of hammering, saw blades, and shouting.

"What is going on?" said Wil, leaning on an elbow and straining to see from his sleeping bag. "It's only six-thirty."

"They're working on the field," said Tara. "Cody and I already went down there and checked it out."

Tom decided to rest as long as he could. They'd been up until midnight at the library, slamming virtual singles, doubles, and a fair amount of pop-up flies, and the images were still flying through his mind.

When, after breakfast, he did manage to reach the ballpark, Tom saw that the parading fans had turned into a crew of fix-it fanatics.

All around the park, one group after another tackled job after job. There was a masonry crew—Mrs. Flores and Graydog—working on fortifying the stone wall with mortar and rock. Another crew worked on replacing boards. Another on tar-patching and recoating the dugout roof timbers. And still another scraped off old, peeling paint from the bleachers, getting ready to recoat the ancient boards. Some painted banners. Some set up booths.

Strangely, more news reporters had shown up as well. The players soon found out why. Somehow, their little battle to preserve the hometown ball field, the surrounding countryside, and the unique character of the town had struck a nerve across the region.

Save Our Forest–type groups of all sorts had been calling talk shows and e-mailing TV stations throughout the Southwest for the past few days to voice their support for the Wildcats and to vent their outrage at the plan.

On the other side, construction workers, business leaders, and politicians lined up to tell the world what a shame it was that, at a time of high housing costs and a housing shortage, a few tree-huggers would not allow this small town to grow.

During a midmorning water break, Tom finally got a chance to check his e-mail. He had over 400 messages from people from all over who'd logged on to the Wildcat website and wanted to send their support.

Never give up! Never surrender! read one. Others were more along the lines of *Tell Dante we still love him* and *It's not the size of the dog in the fight that counts, but the size of the fight in the dog!* He had no time to read them all.

But in the dugout, it was all the players could talk about.

Frankie kept saying, "Tommy, look what you got us into." Then he'd bust up, slap Tom's back, and try to find a camera to strut in front of.

"This reminds me of the county fair," said Rachel. "The noise, the commotion. Only in this fair, we're the animal exhibit."

Outside, behind the dugout, the players could hear Mayor Calabaza arguing with Graydog and several other men.

"None of these improvements have been authorized," said

the mayor. "So don't expect to get reimbursed from the Council for expenses."

"Don't worry," Graydog answered. "We wouldn't expect that—not from people who can't even understand why we're doing this."

Tom recognized Mr. Jones's voice. "Stupidest thing I ever seen. Pouring good money after bad."

María could not sit still. She tossed her water bottle against the dugout wall and marched up the steps, right up to the men, saying, "We don't think it's stupid when people help people out of the goodness of their hearts, which to you, I'm sure, is a foreign concept, and therefore, you have no right to criticize!"

"Well, Sugardoll," Mr. Jones said, nice and slow, "why are you so upset with me?"

Tom could only imagine her wildfire eyes, her finger pointing and jabbing, the fierce look of *la desperada loca,* when María answered.

"Because, you think you're so smart!" she said. "Well, *escuche.* Because there's something amazing happening here, but you don't know what it is, do you, Mr. Jones?"

She didn't wait for an answer. She stomped back to the dugout, glared down at her wide-eyed teammates, and huffed. She snatched her hat off a nail, crammed it on, and began jogging toward the center field gates.

As one, Tom, Rachel, Wil, and Frankie rose up and followed her. Soon the entire team was heading out the gates and toward the running hill.

Stirred with strange feelings he'd never felt before, Tom

ran as if this run, this practice, playing on this team, were life-or-death events. Do or die, like the Big Game itself. And before he knew it, Tom heard himself tell Frankie, "I like María. I like her a lot."

By late Thursday afternoon, that one-time broken-down, weedy, seedy baseball park sparkled from the red, white, and blue scorekeepers booth high in the covered bleachers to the new coat of black enamel on the center field gates.

Mr. Ruiz, who owned the Maple View Market, brought in a big truckload of Mexican mangoes from the desert. He ripped open the boxes and invited everyone to help themselves to the sweet tropical fruit.

"*Mi abuelita* always say," Mr. Ruiz shouted, " 'You cannot fandango until you eat your mango.' So eat up, *mis amigos*, and let the dance begin!"

Soon everyone had fresh mango juice covering their hands and dripping from their elbows. Brassy mariachi music poured out of a CD player. It was the perfect way to end practice and gain the energy needed for a final run down the mountain.

By now all of the workouts felt routine to Tom, second nature. The Christmas lights drill, the hundred ground balls, the hundred flies, baserunning, and bunting drills had all made an impact. Not only on players like Tara and Tom, who still struggled to get their gloves to the ball before the ball hit their toes, but for Frankie and María and Cruz as well.

But the trek down the mountain had registered a special effect. Tom ran with more speed, less hesitation. He could read the whole hillside from the top down. Once he started, he let gravity pull him along, using his feet merely as stabilizers, as steering.

And on today's final run, instead of Cruz finishing far ahead of everyone else, with Tom and Cody bringing up the rear, Tom noticed that Cruz and Rachel and Frankie had run sideways routes, taking more time, so that the team could arrive at the ball field in a pack. And they all talked about their legs feeling stronger, their minds seeming quicker, more alert. They were winded, but easily caught their wind.

And the wind caught them. It held them, rivered around them, joining each one with the others. It was the way, Tom decided, a real team feels.

And this real team stood this late afternoon at second base, eyeing the makeover with strong, but mixed, emotions. "Man, you guys," said Wil. "It looks sweet, but I hope they realize that if we lose, all this work'll be for nothing."

"They realize it," said Rachel. "I heard Graydog tell my mom, 'If we have to bury this field, at least it'll be in a beautiful coffin.'"

Solemnly, they jogged off to the library.

20

"Hollis B! Come on up!" Dodge Bullit stood in the score booth with a microphone at his mouth, introducing the first guest of his Friday show.

"People," he said, "we've gotten a chance to meet a few of the locals around here over the past couple of days, and I want to introduce you to one man who is never at a loss for words."

The Friday lunch crowd swiveled in their seats, scanning the area for Hollis B. Today the group was bigger than ever. Word had gotten around about the spread Maggie and Daisy laid out for the midday meal, and lots of others brought dishes to contribute along with large appetites. Even Del Gato dropped off a huge box this morning, filled with fresh ears of corn, tomatoes, yellow squash, and *habañero* peppers from his garden.

"Here he is," shouted Graydog. "Here's Hollis B!"

Up the far side rail and across the last row of seats, Hollis B gyrated and danced his way to the impromptu radio studio in the score booth. Today, instead of wearing his dark wool skullcap, he wore a Kansas City Royals baseball cap, with a big *KC* on the front, that seemed to give him a formal appearance, as if he were about to testify in church or in court.

"Well, okay, then," said Mr. Bullit. "Come on in. Welcome to the Bullit Train, Mr. B."

"Hollis B, that's me. Not Mr. B. Mr. B, that's my dad. My dead dad. My dad's dead. I could not be a Mr. B. But some people say I'm a Mr. E."

Tom just shook his head and knocked knuckles with Cruz.

"I agree," was all Dodge Bullit could come up with. "Now, then, Hollis B, people also say you're a man of vision."

"Well, I will tell you," he said, his amplified voice rumbling through the stands. "I'm more of a Mantle or a Stengel or a George Herman Ruth. So don't ask me nothing about nothing—I just might tell you the truth."

Over the cheers, Mr. Bullit said, "Well, sir, I hope you do. So tell us, who's going to win the Big Game?"

Hollis B wrinkled up one side of his face, squinting and concentrating.

"Well, I will tell you," he began again. "Now, I got a little concerned we might get burned the first day I saw three good players go, and so I says, when we lose nine, then what'll we do, Mastermind? And I have to actually tell you, I ain't looking to snow or sell you, but in a jingle-jangle world where hope is hype, these Wildcats are more your Jennifer Lopez type. I mean, now from success." He held up a finger. "By playing their cards close to their chest. See, they are being hated, cast down, and berated, by all the big owners and all the negated. But it pays to have a winner in your own home park, just like it pays to have money when the lights go dark."

Hollis B stopped and squinted into the crowd, who sat quietly, waiting. Then he tugged on his cap and said, "I gotta go."

And as if the roar and applause blew him back, he recoiled, sprang up, ducked his head, and slinked out of view.

"Thank you, Hollis B," said Dodge Bullit. "We appreciate your presence here. Now, Mr. de la Cruz, will you come to the microphone?"

Cruz got up without a word. He glanced at Del Gato and held up a reassuring hand as he scaled the bleachers and leaned into the booth.

"Now, young man, do *you* have any observations with reference to the Big Game tomorrow?"

Cruz bent down close to the mike and spoke in a low voice. "Well, I'd say my views are just about the same as Hollis B's."

He stood tall, tipped his cap, and walked back down.

By late Friday afternoon, something else was different. Batting practice. Not on the computers. This time it was real life. Del Gato pitched, and everyone hit. They'd spent hours with the HitSim—swinging and staring and swinging some more—and something had changed.

Today, they hit fastballs and curves, even some of the murderous kind. Cody and Tara slapped the ball with more power. Clifford, Frankie, María, and Rachel smacked it like hitting tennis balls with a racquet. Wil and Ramón reached the warning track some 285 feet away. But Cruz—he was unconscious, driving ball after ball deep into the outfield and up against the stone wall.

Tom felt something strange going on in him, too. No, he didn't hit any rockets or long bombs. His dribblers and pop-ups barely cleared the infield. The difference was in his head.

He tracked the ball better than he ever had. Sometimes he could even see the seams. And he wasn't missing the ball as much with his swings. He was actually making contact.

Fielding improved as well. One hundred ground balls in a row will do that for even the weakest fielder. And one hundred fly balls, day after day, will have a Tara Gleason tracking them down like Barry "U.S." Bonds.

By now, droves of reporters and photographers and television crews roamed the grounds. The dirt roadway cutting through Doc's land and heading to the ballpark was jammed, both sides, with satellite trucks, microwave trucks, radio vans, and SUVs.

All around the ball field, news crews set up lawn chairs, coolers, tripods, and umbrellas.

Some of the townspeople showed up with cookies and ice-cold lemonadeberry tea for the press, serving a few opinions to them as well.

After he'd finished hitting, Tom heard one Los Angeles newscaster begin his interview with Mrs. Gleason by saying, "Folks, something phenomenal is happening in America today. There are more baseball games across the nation tonight than people have seen in years. From little hamlets like this one to the last weed-filled vacant lots in cities everywhere, the Wild West showdown flavor of this Big Game has fired up interest and imaginations all over this land."

"Just focus on your hitting and fielding," Del Gato reminded everyone as the team finished its second round of batting practice. "Hitting, fielding."

Then came the ESPN truck, and the players stopped what they were doing and stared as it all sank in. The Dillontown Wildcats were going *national*.

"Don't pay any attention," Del Gato called from the pitcher's mound. "Crying out loud, they got nothing better to do than hound a bunch of kids?"

Tom hustled out and sat atop the old stone wall in right field, pretending to be taking a break, while he spied on the guy from ESPN.

"How long's he going to pitch, fella?" he asked Tom.

"One more hitter, then we're done."

The reporter turned to a man with a camera on his shoulder, stepping out of the huge white truck. "Roy! Only one more batter. Get down there!" Then he slapped at his shirt pocket, retrieving a notebook and pen. "What's your name, partner? How old are you? What's it like to have a legend like 'El Gato Loco' coaching your squad?"

Tom wanted to answer every question, but the last one reminded him that he needed to stay focused. "Sorry, I can't talk now." Then he couldn't help himself. He had to know. "Is that why you're here? All because of him?"

"Oh, no. Don't you see, kid? This Big Game, your whole situation here, has caught the attention of the entire nation. It's David versus Goliath! It's loyalty versus the big bucks. The small-market team fighting for its life against the big-money boys who want to come in and bulldoze right over them. It's a metaphor for the entire game of baseball."

"It is?"

"I'm telling you, buddy. It's *more* than a metaphor. This could be a meta*five!*"

With that, he stabbed the pen back into his pocket, folded the notebook, and ran toward the cameraman, followed by another guy wrapped in headgear and holding a furry microphone on a pole.

Luckily for the reporter, and for everyone in the stands, the last batter was Cruz. Because he put on a show.

"Ramón," he called out. "This one's for you." On the next pitch, he served up a low line drive into left field, two steps to the right of Ramón.

"María, get ready," he yelled, and the next one, a sharp ground ball, sizzled down the first-base line. María snagged it on the short hop.

The crowd *woo*ed at how easily she made the play.

By the time Cruz called Tom's name and sent him deep against the right-field wall, hoots and whistles rippled out of the stands for both hitter *and* fielder. More than that. Between pitches, Tom now heard a definite buzz of surprise, of discovery and awe.

"What're you feeding 'em for breakfast, Gallagher? A box of Wheaties and a pound of nails?"

Every hitter had done well that day, better than usual. The fielders had all displayed fundamental improvement, even over yesterday. But Cruz's show was full of flair and finesse. He could not miss. Like a pool player, he called his shots, hitting any pitch, high or low, toward any player. Hitting the ball as if it were standing still.

Finally, the awesome display seemed to be sinking into the minds of the fans in the stands, particularly those, like Doc, who'd been there since Monday.

The ballpark became a canyon of quiet, save for Cruz's roll call and the slap of the ball on his maplewood bat. "Frankie, turn two!"

Frankie charged the hot grounder, stabbed it, tossed it to Tara at second, who relayed it to María at first. Smooth as *mole de chocolate*. Again the crowd called out its admiration.

Tom felt a giddy light-headedness as he watched. For the first time, he felt happy to be here. Tara, running back to second, smiled and gave him thumbs-up.

At the end of practice, the low voices in the dugout and the serious looks of quiet confidence on the faces of the other players only confirmed Tom's suspicions that they felt it, too.

"We got half a chance," said Ramón.

"Yeah," added Rachel.

There it was. The team's two quietest players had spoken the words no one else had dared to say.

"Grab all your stuff," Del Gato growled, bringing a bucket of balls in from the mound. "We're going to jog out of here. And if those reporters come swarming around—well, you know the drill."

The players rose and filed out of the dugout. They started through the crowd and back to camp. Except for one. Tom lingered behind, sitting alone on the old pine bench. He wanted to savor the thrill of this moment. He wanted to allow everything that had happened to sink in. He let his thoughts fly loose, like leaves in the wind, like sagebrush whizzing past his face as he ran through the hillside chaparral. Then he reached for the sports bag next to his feet, pulled out his Dreamsketcher, and began to write.

Images of newscasters, landowners, outsiders, and locals who came to root or gloat, hate or berate, filled the movie screen of his mind. He painted the scenes in drawings and word pictures as fast as he could scratch. This awkward, ten-membered, twenty-legged caterpillar of a team, cocooned for days in the school library and on a sunken baseball field, was now breaking out into butterfly beauty, putting on a show, catching everyone's eye.

Tom pushed his pen along the paper, capturing the moment. He could still hear the roar, the drumbeats. He could hear footsteps. He looked up.

There stood Alabaster Jones.

21

Well, Tom Gallagher," he said. "Just the man I'm looking for." He descended the dugout steps. "You boys must think you're pretty smart."

Tom only stared, afraid even to blink or breathe.

"Yes, sir," Mr. Jones continued, "I heard all about what you and that Mexican boy did. Think you're some clever *muchachos*, don't you?"

Tom managed a slight shrug.

Mr. Jones stepped closer, lowering his face into Tom's, and grabbed the neck of his T-shirt. "You ride off and bring back that no-good, drugged-out disgrace of a human being to coach this team of miserable misfits. Get him to sober up for two minutes and show you a little something about hitting. Huh? Speak up!"

"Mr. Del Gato is not a disgrace. He has a lot of grace."

The man twisted his fist, tightening Tom's shirt around his neck.

"Shut up. Now, I'm only saying this once, so listen good. If by hocus or by pocus you happen to win tomorrow and this land deal falls through, you will sincerely regret it. I have associates in this town who promised me that they will personally shut down Scrub Oak Community School, fire the staff, and make all you kids hike down and back each day to that Lake View Mesa school if things don't go as planned.

And why would we do all that? Simple lack of funds, my boy. It's big tax dollars you kids are playing with. Big money all around. Do you understand?"

He did. Instantly, Tom could see a whole chain of events, like dominoes falling whap-slap into each other. Either the Wildcats lose tomorrow, or Tom's parents lose their jobs. Then maybe even their home.

Compared to that, a few houses up on the hill didn't seem so bad.

Mr. Jones must've read the understanding on Tom's face. He let go of his shirt and smiled.

"Good," he said. "Because I can cause you more hurt than a heart attack." He grinned so wide, his sunburned lips turned white.

Tom stared back, blinking hard. But if Tom had learned anything during the past week, he'd learned when he had to speak up and when it was better to be silent.

And now was a time to speak.

"We're not trying to hurt you," said Tom. "We don't have anything against you at all. Why are you trying to hurt us?"

"Oh, you poor, poor boy. Listen, if you win that game, you'll be hurting me far more than what I could ever do to you. And I mean right here." He tapped his white sports jacket on the left side of his chest. "In my wallet."

Then Mr. Jones's face seemed to change, turning softer. Worry rose in his eyes. "You see, son, I was once a lot like you. I was young. I had stars in my eyes. But what you don't understand is that in the game of life, money wins. Brains can only take you so far. Talent barely gets you in the door these days. But this"—he held up his hand and rubbed his thumb against his first two fingers—"this opens more doors than dynamite. With this, you have instant respect, instant power."

Mr. Jones turned, but he did not leave. He looked off toward Rattlesnake Ridge as if imagining what all this land would be like after he was done with it.

"Remember," he said, "without money and the wish for even more money, Columbus never would've sailed to America. Then where would we all be today? Think about that."

Under the stars that Friday night, all of the players joined in the wheel-spoke circle, and all eyes were wide open. Who could sleep with the weight of the fate of the town squeezing down on them?

Okay, Wil could. But he'd had three *burritos grandes,* four slices of watermelon, and a mango after catching batting practice all afternoon.

"No one expects us to win," said Clifford, lying with his knees up and hands behind his head. "I think somebody's going to be real surprised."

Ramón agreed. "My dad came by this morning saying, 'Don't worry. This game doesn't even matter. Sooner or later this whole place will be houses and eight-lane freeways.' I just smiled and said, 'Yeah, Dad, we know.' "

"That's what the mayor said, too," Frankie added. "But when he was watching batting practice today, he was white as a tortilla."

"Yeah," Cruz agreed. "But I think his true color was *Alabaster*. Right, María? What are you going to say to him after we ruin his plans?"

Tom's gut clenched.

"Hey, look, you guys," María answered. "Don't get overconfident. Remember, batting practice is one thing. But in a game—especially this one—it's different. There's a lot of pressure."

"She's right," said Ramón. "But I think Cruz and Clifford are, too. The way I see it, as long as we think we have a chance, we have a chance."

Tom kept silent. His mind was still frozen under the snake eyes of a man named Jones who loomed above him like a viper over a rat. What did he expect Tom to do? Tell Cruz and everyone to throw the game? Tom was just the bench guy, the reserve player. Even if he got into the game, which would only happen if one team was way ahead of the other, he could strike out and make an error or two, but big deal. It would hardly affect the game.

Maybe, he thought, he could coach first and trip everyone as they ran the bases. Or maybe he could go out to the score-board with a mirror and shine sunlight into all the batters' eyes. But he hated these thoughts. In fact, he was tired of thinking.

"Tom," said Cruz. "What do you think?"

Boom went his heartbeat.

"About what?"

"About the neural receptors inside our brains."

"What?"

"Okay, then. Are we going to win tomorrow?"

"Oh. I don't know. It's up to you guys."

"Aaapp!" said Frankie. "Wrong answer."

"Well, he *doesn't* know." It was María coming to Tom's de-fense. "No one does. We spent three days swinging at the same stupid pitch a million times. But it was in the *library*. What about real life?"

"What about it?" asked Clifford. "You saw us today. We smashed the chips-and-dip out of the ball."

"So?" Rachel rustled inside her bag as she flipped over to her stomach. "I mean, I don't know what happened to us in the library. If we got hypnotized or reprogrammed or brainwashed or what. All I know is, we can't forget we're human beings. And humans have control over their thoughts. And as long as we concentrate on doing our best, we shouldn't worry about winning or losing."

She paused, her voice lowered to a whisper. "I just believe that when people do things with good intentions, good things happen. Like when Tom and Cruz rode off to see Del Gato. But when we do stuff out of fear, bad things happen." She looked around. "A lot of people are afraid of what might happen tomorrow. But *we* can't be. Then, whatever happens will turn out okay."

"Even if we lose?" asked Frankie.

"Even if we lose. I mean, from where we are, losing may look like a total disaster. Like we just accidentally busted down somebody's wall." Though he couldn't see her, Tom could hear the smile in her voice. "But you know, we only see it from here. How does it look from the hawk's nest? Or from the stars?"

No one said a word. Everyone, even Tom, searched the night sky, roamed the ether, bouncing around between the moon, the stars, and the eucalyptus trees.

From treetop, from the hawk's perch, Tom thought about the game, the town, the hillsides. In a million years—a short time, really, in space years—would it even matter whether they won or lost? In a thousand? What about a hundred?

Who could say? But he knew one thing. Rachel was right. He'd seen it too many times. When he froze up from fear, he did stupid things—like never talking to Doc about the ball field. And when he let his mind fly above the fear, he saw hitting a baseball as just another form of GPS tracking.

No matter if his parents got fired and his family had to move. No matter what trouble Alabaster Jones might cause, Tom determined that tomorrow he would play to win. And now he wondered how he could've considered doing anything else.

As the team let their thoughts drift and dance beneath the diamond sky, on their way to sleep, Cruz had the last word. "Rachel," he whispered. "Will you run away with me?"

There was no response beyond low hums and squirms, because everyone knew what he meant. And Tom fell asleep wondering what the red-tailed hawk might think, looking down and seeing ten smiles beneath the pepper tree.

Hey, you guys!"

It was Cody, running and sliding into the sleeping-bag circle, the only one awake on the only morning the players were allowed to sleep in.

"Tom, get up! All you guys, wake up. Cruz is gone!"

"What?" Tom rolled from his side to his stomach and lifted his head.

"He's gone," Cody repeated. "His duffel bag's gone, Screwball's gone. His sleeping bag is all rolled up and put away on the bunkhouse shelf."

"He's not gone," said Wil. "Not *gone* gone. He probably just went out for a ride."

"He'll be back," said Frankie. "Get some more sleep, little guy."

Cody knelt on Tom's bag and whispered, "Tom, I think he really is."

"How do you know?"

"Why would he take everything, all his gear, and leave his uniform?"

Now Tom sat up, looking into the morning light. He yawned and stretched. Cruz could not possibly be gone, he thought. Where would he go? And why?

"Let me see." Tom slipped on his sandals and started for the bunkhouse and barn. Then he stopped as he remembered

Cruz's final words last night. Slowly, he turned to see if Rachel was still there.

Well, of course she is, he thought as he saw her, still resting, with an arm across her eyes. Cruz wouldn't run away.

Inside the barn, he stared at Screwball's empty stall, raked and cleaned. And instantly he knew. He felt it in his bones. Yes, he was gone.

"Why would he do this?" Tom mumbled.

"He's the Death and Doom guy," said Cody. "That's why."

Tom stared at Cody a moment, then looked back at the stall. He could not talk. When he felt his throat swell up, he kicked a pail of nuts and bolts, sending hardware flying everywhere.

No! he thought. No, this cannot be happening!

Then he forced out a scream. Rushing to the back of the barn, he yanked his saddle off its post. "Cody, I'm leaving! I'm going after him." He gathered his riding gear, looping the bridle reins over his shoulder.

"You know where he is, Tom? Where?"

"I don't know. How should I know? I just have to go look."

"No, you don't." María, her arms folded, still groggy from sleep, had wandered through the doorway. "He's gone. I saw him go." She kept coming, shaking as if she were cold. "I mean, not really. But I dreamed it. I dreamed he came walking through the baseball field, leading his horse. And he just walked right on by. It was the weirdest thing. He was smiling."

"But that's just a dream, María." Tom hoisted his saddle. "I can't—"

She grabbed his arm. "To you, maybe. But, Tom, I know. These things can happen. Because when I woke up, I still knew."

Cody jumped up and ran out of the barn, yelling, "María had a dream, you guys, that Cruz is really gone! She dreamed it!"

María ignored him. "Besides, even if I'm wrong, where are you going to look? He's probably two or three hours ahead of you by now."

Tom lowered the saddle to the ground and knelt on it. "I don't know," he said. "I don't know anything."

The scene at the field on Saturday morning was crazy. Parked cars and double-parked cars lined both sides of the highway leading into town. RVs, SUVs, and pickup trucks filled Doc's lower field.

News reporters scurried around asking for Del Gato, who should've been there, Tom figured, but it was only ten-thirty, and the game wouldn't start until noon. Still, where was he?

No, thought Tom, *no*. They can't both disappear.

"Coach Gallagher?" asked one TV reporter, as the team headed for the field, passing the grandstands. "We'd like an interview with the boy from Paloma. We ran a tape last night of his hitting exhibition, and we got flooded with calls. Other stations want more footage and more background."

"He's not here." Tom's dad hurried his step.

The reporter stopped, stunned. Then he shouted, "What about the HitSim game? What can you tell us about that?"

Tom nudged Frankie. "They already know about the Hit-Sim?"

"It was in the paper this morning. I think Wil's dad told them."

Mr. and Mrs. Gallagher hustled the team onto the field.

"We can't worry any more about Cruz," Mr. Gallagher told the players as they gathered in the dugout. "We're trying to reach his mother. But he'll either be here by game time or he won't. Right now, it looks like we'll have to plan on playing without him."

"But who's going to pitch?" asked Cody. "We'll get shredded."

"You guys!" María yelled, standing at the end of the dugout. "We can't get all stupid over this. It's just like the first day of camp. We play with whoever shows up. If Cruz wants to 'Cruz on,' or some dumb thing, then let him. I don't like quitters. And if Del Gato flakes—" For a moment she seemed flustered. Her hands flicked and fluttered above her head. "—Hey, we can't be worried about that, either. We got a game to play." She turned her glare to the ball field and fell back onto the bench.

Tom's dad rubbed the back of his neck. "Yeah, well, María's right. We'll figure something out. Frankie has a good arm. So does Ramón. Once Mr. Del Gato gets here, and I hope to gosh he does, we'll put a plan together. Until then, stay cool."

In the stands, people ran around stringing up banners, bunting, and signs. Tom watched Wil's dad and mom hang one that read, *Go Wildcats!! Where there's a Wil, there's a way.* One banner already strung along the rooftop said, *We Were Country Before the Country Was Full!* All around, men pushed carts and dragged wagons filled with boxes of food and drinks.

Looking over the top of the dugout, Tom saw Mrs. Flores directing traffic. She had a whistle around her neck that she clutched in one hand while holding a clipboard in the other.

"No, Hector!" she yelled at her oldest son. "Don't set up there. Goat meat and flatbread belong on the other side with the other food stands."

Then Tom spotted his mother and Maggie walking up with Del Gato. He never thought he would be so happy to see that man.

In fact, Del Gato looked better than ever. A haircut! Tom realized. Is that why he was late? He'd stopped by Maggie's for a haircut and a shave?

Del Gato rounded the corner of the dugout, into everyone's view, and the whole team cheered. María curled her tongue and whistled, two long tones, a wolf whistle. Then everyone laughed, as they, too, realized Del Gato had gotten cleaned up for the game.

"Hey, no glitter on the 'do?" asked Frankie. "No blue tips?"

"Ah, geez." Del Gato lifted his hat to show off Maggie's work. "Give a guy a break. I told her no blue dye until after the game—if we win."

The dugout exploded in a roar. For a moment it seemed they'd all forgotten about Cruz. Except Tom. He still hoped Cruz would show up. Not just because the team really needed him, but because Tom did. Once the dugout had re-settled, Tom's dad turned to him and said, "You're in the starting lineup now. So get ready."

Tom froze. He had completely forgotten that.

I can't, I can't, I can't, he thought. I *can't* go out there. I'll be horrible. I'll make us lose. He plopped himself down on the end of the bench. A blur invaded his mind. "I can't," he finally said.

The dugout went silent. Tom felt the eyes of every player in it focus on him.

"Why not?" his father asked.

The words were gone. All the little steps he'd taken all week long seemed to have gone backwards in one second. He began to shake. He tightened his arms and legs against the shaking, but it only made him shake worse.

When he sensed Del Gato alongside him on the pine plank, a hot wave of embarrassment rained down on him.

Del Gato addressed the team. "You guys give us a minute?"

Tom's dad answered. "Let's loosen up, everyone. Grab your gloves."

The players sprinted onto the field.

Del Gato did not look at Tom. He folded his arms and spoke toward the low retaining wall at the foot of the dugout.

"The other night at Doc's," he started, "I left something out of my story. One week after I quit baseball, I got the shock of my life. I found out that the level I'd taken my hitting to in the play-offs was only temporary. That it was the kind of deal you had to work on every day just to keep it going."

Well, thought Tom, at least you got there. You got to be perfect.

Del Gato picked up Tom's maplewood bat from the floor. Tom had brought it to show to Cruz. Del Gato stood, flipped the bat sideways from hand to hand. Still, he addressed the field.

"See, by the time the play-offs started, I was working at a froth. Then something just clicked, and bam! My brain jumped into overdrive. But no way could I've kept that work-out pace up for a full season." He swiveled and looked directly at Tom. "Which means, I quit for nothing."

Finally, Tom took a breath. "You did?"

Del Gato sat down on the second step, drew up his legs, and rested on them. "I didn't have any magic secret," he said. "I mean, I did, but it wasn't locked in the way I thought it was. Man, I got a sick feeling when I realized that. 'Course, by then, I couldn't go back. I mean, who'd believe me or even want me after what I'd done to the Padres? Besides, I *was* a drunk. At least, I had been. And right away I went back to it."

That surprised Tom. "Then that stuff everybody says is true?"

"A lot of it was, until a couple years ago. Doc finally got me squared away. But that's between me and you, huh?"

Tom gave a hard, firm nod.

"You want to end up like me, fine. Quit. But you're a special guy, Tom. You got heart. I saw that the first time you ran down the mountain." He tilted his head. "Might not be the most coordinated kid on the block, but you got heart. And one thing I have learned is, guys with heart shouldn't quit. Because if they do, it disappears."

Heart? Tom let the word echo inside. He thinks I've got heart? Just hearing that seemed to calm him a little. "But I'm just a number-nine hitter. You make me sound like—"

"Nine? I got you batting seventh."

"You do?"

"I liked what I saw yesterday."

"You did?"

"Hey, Tom, I need you, all right? Listen, you do this for me, and I'll let you patch up my broken wall."

Tom looked up and tightened his bottom lip to keep from smiling.

"Not only that," Del Gato continued, "I'll teach you how to live all alone up on a mountaintop, how to dream up your own cusswords, and how to growl like a dog. Sound fair?"

"Yeah," said Tom, rising and breaking into a full grin. "Sounds real fair."

Del Gato humphed and slapped the bill of Tom's cap. "Then get out there. I'm tired of looking at you."

A half hour before game time, the whole park was jammed with people. Old people on lawn chairs rimmed the side fences, families on blankets and beach towels filled the embankments, and the stands were packed. Tom figured a thousand people were there. But still no Cruz.

Both teams lined up behind the center field gates. Don Robledo's Mariachi Marching Band, five musicians dressed in black short-waist jackets and gold-buttoned pants, blasted their trumpets and strummed their guitars and the fat *gui-tarrón*. The teams followed them in, marching onto the field.

Women dressed in *las trajes*, in red ruffled skirts and white blouses, danced alongside the band—a sight Tom had grown up with, but he wondered what the Viking players were thinking.

Up in the score booth, Mayor Calabaza was in his glory, standing up, shouting into the microphone, announcing the starting lineups to the crowd.

Frankie would lead off, followed by María and Ramón. Wil would bat cleanup, ahead of Clifford and Rachel. Tom, Tara, and Cody would hit at the bottom of the order.

The biggest surprise, though, was pure Del Gato. And to Tom, it was genius. Instead of having Tom take over in right field, where he was usually banished, Cody would play right, and Tom would play first base. It was a position Tom had played before, and it demanded the least amount of running and throwing, so it made a bit of sense. And why the big change?

Because on the mound, it would not be Frankie or Ramón. The starting pitcher for the Big Game was María.

Her first question was, "Is it legal? Do they let you pitch underhand in baseball?"

"Why not?" Del Gato answered. "Who's going to stop you?"

"I don't know."

"Just do what you did the other day. Crying out crickets." He turned serious again. "You're a pitcher, aren't you?"

María squeezed her eyes shut. "Yeah, I guess."

Del Gato grumbled as he walked away.

Once the Wildcats finished their round of infield practice, they ran in, and Tom felt relieved to be back in the dugout.

"Are you nervous?" he asked Rachel, sitting next to him.

"Nervous?" She leaned on her knees. "My butterflies have butterflies. I think I might puke."

"Ah," said María, touching them both on the shoulder. "You mean I'm not the only one?" Tom didn't look up, but he felt a reassuring calm from her fingers.

Del Gato stood on the steps and clapped his hands. "Okay, we're the home team, so we take the field first." He glanced left and right, obviously, thought Tom, looking one last time for Cruz. Then he ducked his head and stepped down into the dugout. "All right, gather up."

The players assembled into a circle. "Everyone, just take a deep breath. Be alert out there, look ahead, and think ahead. Because the deal is, we got one more mountain to run down. All right?" He held out his hand. The players all reached in and set their hands on top of his. "Wildcats, run," he said. "On three. *Uno, dos, tres.*"

"WILDCATS, RUN!"

They screamed the words as loud as they could. Then, to a thunder-crack roar and a standing ovation, they sprinted out of the dugout and onto the field. Tom could not even feel his feet touch the earth or the ball in his hand. Rachel took a detour on her way to center field, stopping near the right field foul pole to quietly and politely puke.

24

While throwing warm-up grounders to the infielders, Tom couldn't help but notice Hollis B standing on the edge of the Wildcats' dugout roof. Facing sideways toward the band, which now sat in the middle of the stands, Hollis B waved his cell phone up and down and threw his head back and forth, as if conducting the brassy music.

By the time the tune ended, the veins on Hollis B's neck stood out red and bulging. "I ain't fakin'!" he screamed. "*Whole* lotta shakin' goin' on!"

The crowd responded with another fierce burst. The impact of their voices was so strong, Hollis B ran to the far end of the dugout, jumped off, and kept running all the way down the right field line.

From shortstop, Frankie turned and yelled, "Hollis B, you rock!"

Hollis B stood at attention, dropped his phone into the pocket of his sleeveless blue work shirt, and saluted. Every Wildcat saluted back.

María began her warm-up tosses, and the Viking players began to heckle. "Hey, this ain't girls' softball," yelled one guy. "Stand up there and pitch like a man!"

The hoots and wails from the dugout came fast and delirious.

"Yo, my sister wants to play!" another one yelled. "But she

has to baby-sit a bunch of little kids. Oh, wait a minute, there she is now—standing in center field!"

More laughs and jeers, from the fans as well. Tom hated to see what María was going through. But Tom should've known what the Vikings didn't. They should not have picked on Rachel *or* María.

"She ain't your sister, Zit Head," María yelled back. "Your sister has four legs and a leash, just like *tu madre!*"

Don Robledo started up the band, drowning out any more cross-dugout repartee.

All of the attention on María actually seemed to relax her. And after a dozen warm-up tosses, she had her rhythm and her form. Her final toss snapped against Wil's mitt like a bull-whip crack.

"Batter up," called the ump. "Play ball!"

María turned and faced her teammates from the mound. "Okay, you guys. Focus!"

The mayor, still standing since the score booth was jammed with reporters, announced the Vikings' leadoff hitter. A tall lefty sauntered up to the plate, looking back at his teammates and wearing a silly smirk.

María's first pitch was a blazing fastball, right at the batter's head. The crowd gave out a loud cry, and Lefty hit the dirt.

Frankie punched his glove with a loud smack. "*Bien-venidos a* Dillontown," he said.

The next pitch was low and away, and the batter fouled it off. It was the only pitch touched by a Viking bat in that inning.

María mowed them down. They had no clue. Her delivery

was completely foreign to them, not to mention the strange movement on the ball. Three up, three down, three strike-outs. At the end of the inning, Wil whipped off his mask and ran out to tell everyone, "Her ball's really rising! Did you see it? It's going straight up! I'm not kidding. Those guys were swinging at a black hole!"

If someone had told Tom that the only hit for either team during the first three innings would be Tara's line-drive single to center, he would have suggested a mental exam. But here it was, halfway through this six-inning game, and the score was tied, 0–0.

"What are we doing wrong?" said Wil. "Nobody's making solid contact. I can see that stupid pitch of his in my sleep, but when I stand up there, it's not quite the same. I'm just nicking it."

"We all are," said Ramón. "That's why we're popping up and grounding out."

"Not Tara. How'd you do it, Tara?"

"I don't know. I got a pitch that looked a lot like the ones on the computer and I just timed it right, I guess."

"It'll come," said Del Gato. "To all of you. Don't think too much. Let the automatic part of your brain do the work. Next time through the batting order, you'll do better."

Well, they would *have* to do better. In the top of the fourth inning, the Vikings began to connect.

With one out and nobody on, María threw a low fastball that the batter blasted right up the middle, right back at her. With lightning reflexes, she dropped her glove to her shoe, just ahead of the ball. But as it bounced in front of the mound, it took a sharp, wicked hop away from her glove and right into her shinbone.

Thwack! An ugly sound.

The crowd *oohh*ed in sympathy as the ball shot off into foul territory. Wil tracked it down, but he had no play. The Vikings had their first base runner, and the Wildcats had a one-legged pitcher.

Del Gato rushed onto the field, followed by Tom's dad. María sat on the mound, clutching her shin.

"Are you all right?" asked Mr. Gallagher.

"Yeah, yeah, I'm okay. I'll be all right."

Tom's mother was already on the way out with her first-aid kit and an ice pack.

What María had not said was what everyone else had on their minds. She *had* to be all right. She had to stay in the game. If the Wildcats lost even one more player, they'd have to forfeit. They had no one in reserve.

When Mrs. Gallagher touched the ice to her leg, María sucked in a hard breath. "Ahh, feels good," she said through clenched teeth. "Yeah, I'll be *mucho muy* fine."

No one believed her.

"Sit right there a minute," said Del Gato. "Let the ice work." He turned to Tom's dad. "Who else can pitch? Frankie? Ramón?"

"Me?" said Frankie. "I can't pitch."

María leaned back on her arms and squinted up at Del Gato. "No, no. I can do it. Let me take some practice throws. It feels numb already."

She pushed herself up, this time looking steadier. "Where's the ball?" Wil flipped her the baseball.

She threw as hard as ever, but she ended up hopping on her right leg on each follow-through.

"What do you think?" Del Gato asked her.

"I said I'm all right." She turned away from him.

The umpire stepped up. "What's the verdict, folks?"

Del Gato was already leaving. "She's good."

The umpire spun around. "Let's play ball."

The next batter drove a 2-0 fastball into left-center, putting Viking runners on first and third with nobody out.

María bent over, her hands on her knees, obviously in pain. Even so, she pushed herself up and kept pitching. The next batter chopped a sinker up the middle, past Frankie's lunge and into center field, driving in a run. The Vikings now led, 1–0, with runners again on first and third.

The Lake View fans stomped and yelled. Outnumbered about ten to one, they still filled the park with their air horns, claps, and cheers.

Tom peeked out under his cap brim at María. She put both hands on her hips, kicked the pitching mound with her sore leg, sending dust Tom's way in the rising breeze. "We hold them here, you guys!"

Her next pitch was another fastball, low and away. The right-handed batter swung late, hitting a belt-high line drive right to Tom at first base.

The strange thing was, Tom not only saw the ball speeding at him, he saw the spin. To the left, like a curveball. He hardly had to move his feet, but he stretched out his glove and caught the ball in midair. It smacked into the leather with such force that it moved his whole arm backward—and right into the runner who'd darted off first at the crack of the bat.

Catch, tag, *double play*! Tom could not believe it. He jogged off the field realizing something in his brain had changed. Or was it just the wind that had blown the ball his way? At any rate, the inning was over, and they were only one run behind.

Frankie led off the bottom of the fourth with a single to left. María followed with a bunt down the third-base line that went for a hit. Just like Del Gato had predicted, the second time through started producing better results. After Rámon cracked a murveball line drive that the shortstop barely snagged for the first out, Lemanski went to his fastball. That was perfect for Wil, the next batter, a dead fastball hitter.

Maybe it was the HitSim training, maybe the hours of batting practice, or maybe it was the Christmas lights, but Wil seemed to read and meet the ball perfectly. With two runners on, he hit a 1–1 fastball over the stone wall, 300 feet away. Home run! Just like that, the Wildcats shot ahead, 3–1.

They threatened again that inning when Clifford got a one-out single and Rachel got a walk, putting runners at first and second. But Tom struck out swinging and, after a walk to Tara, Cody followed with a soft come-backer to the pitcher. The rally had fizzled.

Before she left the dugout, María rolled up her pant leg, and everyone could see that her shinbone was Damage Central. It looked like someone had injected a purple golf ball just under the surface of her skin. Still, she'd been able to get a good ten minutes of icing on it, and when she started pitching again, she was in top form.

The fans rose to their feet and shouted each time the mariachi trumpeters led them in cheers of "Charge!" But during both halves of the fifth inning, it was the pitchers who were in charge. Neither team scored, and the Wildcats went into the sixth and final frame still out ahead, 3–1.

All María had to do in the top of the sixth in order for the Wildcats to save Dillontown was to hold the Vikings in check and get three outs.

And she would've done it, if her leg would've held her. But the pain grew stronger than the ice could numb. After she walked the first two hitters, the next batter singled in a run, and the guy behind him crushed a double to left that drove in two more. Her edge was gone, and in a blink, the Vikings had pulled ahead, 4–3.

Soon María was joined on the mound by all three coaches.

"I'm okay," she protested, waving them off. But when Tom and Frankie arrived, her lips were pinched pale, her jaw trembled, and her eyes were moist with tears.

It crushed Tom to see her like that, to see that María the fighter could not go on. But now what? If she left the game, the game was over. If Frankie pitched, who'd play short? If Ramón pitched, who'd play left? And what position could María play on one leg?

Tom searched the horizon for Cruz, though by now it was just wishful thinking. Del Gato scanned the entire field, as if looking for ideas. Then their eyes met, and Tom got one—a wild idea.

While Mrs. Gallagher taped an ice pack onto María's shin, Tom bent down and scooped up a handful of dirt. He tossed it straight up and watched. The dust drifted toward first base. To the east.

And he had his answer.

"Mr. Del Gato," he said. "I want to pitch."

"What?" asked Frankie.

Del Gato narrowed his eyes. He was in laser mode.

"Look," said Tom. "I'm the worst fielder out here. I'll do the least harm if I pitch—as long as I keep the ball low and get it over." He could hardly believe he was saying this. "What if María goes to first base? That's her natural spot, and she wouldn't have to run all that much. Then if I pitch, everyone else can stay where they are, at their strongest positions."

Del Gato glanced around the field.

Immediately, Tom had fierce, gut-jangling doubts. His knees gave. What am I thinking? What am I doing? he wondered. Then he decided not to think. He decided to let the automatic part of his brain take over.

"We can do this," he said. "We've got the heart."

"Sounds good to me," said Del Gato. "Warm up. See how you look."

He looked like an idiot, Tom was sure. But he warmed up anyway, starting off with fastballs—if you could call them that—and getting his rhythm—if you could call it that. As he did, he thought about Cruz and the spot he'd left Tom and the whole team in. He threw even harder.

Then he tossed his first cross-fire hurricane.

In a gruff whisper, Del Gato said, "Let me see that again."

Once more, Tom dipped down sidearm and launched a pitch that crossed from the right-handed batter's box to the far corner of the plate, knee high.

"Cheese, Louise." Del Gato rubbed his mouth. "Throw a bunch of them," he said, and left.

When the game resumed, Tom threw a bunch of them, threw enough to cause two ground-ball dribblers, which Clifford and Frankie turned into easy outs, and a called strike three. The inning ended with no more damage. But the Wildcats had only three outs left, and they were down by a run.

A lot depends upon the wind.

Seeds. Spiders. Hawks. Fire. That's just to name a few. The wind carves the earth the same way water does, flowing over mountains, down valleys, carving out canyons and caves, eroding cliffs, transporting sand hundreds of miles away, moving flora and fauna even farther still.

It was this carving that had always fascinated Tom Gallagher. But not until recently had he learned that his brain could be carved, too. Again and again. Carved by currents of thought.

Could thought, then, be the wind of the mind? Could wind, therefore, be the thought of the earth?

He didn't know. But he liked thinking about it.

Frankie led off the bottom of the sixth with the longest double Tom had ever seen. It was a rocket down the left-field line that hit the stone wall, then bounced halfway back to third base.

The hometown fans went into hysterics. No one out, tying run on second, and María, representing the winning run, was up. But she was not there to win the game. On the first pitch, María laid down a sacrifice bunt. Lemanski ran up and gloved it, looked at Frankie steaming to third, but had no play on him, so he got the easy out at first as María limped down the line.

When the next batter, Ramón, looked for a sign, Del Gato simply yelled, "Swing away! Take your best cut."

His best cut sent the next pitch flaring off into left field, a low line drive that looked as if it might fall in. But the left fielder caught it on the run, just above his shoe, and Frankie could not tag up and score on the play.

Now they were down to their final out.

Wil, who'd hit a homer last time up, dug into the box. Only this time, the first pitch was a murveball that didn't murve. It spun and spun, but didn't break, and bounced off the top of Wil's helmet. He ran to first as if he were beating out a bunt. And now, with two outs and two runners on, the crowd went *loco* as Clifford strolled to the plate. Bells, horns, cheers, and drums.

Poor guy, thought Tom. He shook just watching Clifford's arms stiffen as he approached the batter's box in that storm of noise.

"I can't watch this," said Rámon—though he kept watching.

The whole team gathered on the steps, standing or kneeling. And it took only two pitches, a called strike and a foul tip, to put Clifford deep in the hole, 0–2. He stepped away from the plate, swung the bat a few times, trying to loosen up. Tom figured there must've been a thousand prayers rising to heaven from that ballpark, all at once, all put into different words, but most would be addressing the pure fact that there was now only one strike left between hope and a bulldozer.

Clifford walked back into the box. He bent forward and tapped the head of the bat on the plate. Then he got set, staring—glaring—out toward the mound.

Lemanski wound up and sailed a fastball straight at Clifford's fists. But he read it easily, lifting his hands, and leaving the catcher to snag it.

"Ball one!"

Now the fans used their feet, stomping in a slow, steady beat. *Whum-wum, whum-wum, whum-wum, whum!*

A stronger wind began to blow. It began to swirl, swirling up dust, and the drumming came even louder.

Boom-lay, boom-lay, boom-lay boom!

Lemanski leaned in, squinted, took his sign from the catcher, and nodded. Clifford dug a toehold with his back foot. As Lemanski checked the runner on third, it seemed to Tom that the infield dirt began to dance, sending up a williwaw of dust and grit.

Tom realized it was lucky he'd pitched last inning, when the breeze was just right. No way could he have pitched in this crazy squall.

Then Lemanski delivered. It was a drop-down, low-down murveball that did not react like any pitch any of them had seen on the HitSim.

Somehow, at the last instant, a wild gust had put *downward* pressure on the ball. Even Tom felt it.

Clifford started his swing, and even though he tried to

hold back halfway through it, his bat kept going and missed the ball just as it kissed the dirt.

"Strike three!" yelled the umpire, punching the air with his right fist.

Tom pulled his hat over his eyes and sat back down on the bench. That was it. That was it. Bring on the bulldozers.

Then Rachel, María, Ramón, and Tara exploded at once. "Go!" they shouted. "He dropped it! Run!"

Tom pulled off his hat and sprang from the bench.

Lemanski, it seemed, had outfoxed himself. Sure, the pitch was virtually unhittable, but he didn't count on it being uncatchable. Especially in that wind. And now Tom remembered that the catcher *must* catch the third strike, or the batter is free to run.

As the ball rolled all the way to the backstop, Clifford darted down the first-base line, and Frankie scrambled home from third and scored.

Tie game! Safe all around! Clifford had reached first, and Wil had run all the way to third.

Tom looked into the sky, as if something up there would explain the wind that had swooped down out of nowhere. He saw nothing but a few clouds and a red-tailed hawk circling the field, riding an updraft. He just shook his head, then walked to the bat rack as Rachel approached the plate.

Poor Rachel, thought Tom. But he quickly noted, *Better her than me.*

As he slid his bat from the rack and made his way to the

on-deck circle, Rachel strode into that furious wail of cheers, thunder, and trumpets.

"Come on, Rachel!" he called.

Wil, representing the winning run, stood on third base. Over on first, Clifford clapped and yelled. And now, with two outs, it was all up to the strong, quiet center fielder.

"You can do it," screamed Wil. Then he said something else, but it was swallowed up in the cloud of noise.

Relax, Rachel, prayed Tom. *Just relax.*

"Play ball!" cried the ump.

And from the safety of the on-deck circle, Tom watched— in sheer horror—as the catcher rose up, extended his arm, and held four fingers in the air.

Tom spun around to his mom and all the players on the bench. "They're going to walk her!" he yelled. "On purpose!"

He swung his weighted bat as hard as he could. Of course! he realized. They want to load the bases so there'll be a force out anywhere.

And then they want to pitch to me!

He could not feel his hands. He could not feel his toes. Tom took the hugest breath he'd ever drawn. And even that wasn't enough.

"Tom!" Frankie ran up holding the bat Doc had made. "Use this."

"No, I can't. It's too light."

"I know," said Frankie. "That's what I mean. E equals MC squared, *vato*. A faster swing is more important, remember?" Reluctantly, Tom took the bat.

When he heard "Ball four," Tom shuffled or floated or somehow drifted up to home plate. From the first-base coach's box, Mr. Gallagher clapped and shouted as loud as he could. "Focus, Tom. Focus."

Dad, he thought. Don't tell me that. I can't focus and think about focusing at the same time.

"Tommy!" Wil shouted from third base, clapping his hands as fast as he could. "Tommy, baby. Relax. Have some fun."

This is *not* fun, Tom decided. This is the very opposite of fun.

Tom stepped back, squeezing the bat as hard as he could, then loosened and stretched his fingers, trying to relax. Standing there in the middle of the roar, the stomping, the cowbells and trumpets, all Tom could think was, If I strike out, it's okay, it's okay. The game will still be tied, 4–4.

Then he remembered. But I'd still have to pitch. *And* shut them down.

Closing his eyes, he could see the trajectory of the sidearm murve. How it would leave Lemanski's hand, coming right at his ribs, then break sharply down and over the inside corner of the plate. He set his feet in the box accordingly, lowered his hands a little, and stood ready, waiting.

Lemanski fired. Tom read it instantly. Sidearm murve. He read the arc and the speed, and he swung Doc's bat with all his might. It felt great.

Trouble was, the bat was so light that Tom wound up swinging way too early—way out ahead of the pitch. He hit nothing but air.

The crowd reacted with a groan so strong, it suggested to Tom that they saw more than strike one. It was as though they could see strike three.

Tom stepped out of the batter's box and took in a deep breath, forcing himself to calm down. And to slow down. He held up the twenty-nine-inch bat and fingered its smooth handle, remembering the day it was made, remembering the thick, rough-cut branch it had once been before Doc started spinning it on his electric lathe.

On the mound, Lemanski bounced his glove against his thigh, antsy to fire off the next pitch. Tom stepped back in the box, ready. Fortified. For now he realized that he held a part of the mountain in his hands.

As Lemanski went into his windup, Tom's focus was complete. He saw the ball perfectly as it left the pitcher's hand—it was headed for the middle of the plate, just below the waist. Once again, Tom swung. And this time he connected.

But right away he knew his swing had been a tick too soon, and he'd undercut the ball. It was not solid contact.

The finest, fastest, strongest swing he had ever made had resulted only in a pop-up. A Major League pop-up.

The third baseman ran for it, the catcher ran for it, and between them both, the pitcher ran for it, as the ball shot high above the infield, about halfway up the third-base line.

"I got it," called Lemanski.

"No, I got it!" called the catcher. But Tom had hit the ball so hard, it rose above the grandstand roof. And it had so much spin that when it hit the wind up there, it seemed to have a mind of its own, and drifted back toward shortstop.

"Run!" Tom's dad shouted.

"Everybody, run!" screamed Del Gato. Tom scrambled down the first-base line. Wil trotted home. Clifford and Rachel took off like slapped horses.

The third baseman backtracked, calling for the ball, but who could hear? That's when he collided with the shortstop.

That's when Lemanski, looking skyward, tripped and fell on top of them both. That's when the catcher yelled, "Somebody, catch it!"

Nobody did. At least not until after it bounced high above them all and the left fielder scooped it up on the run.

But by then it was all over. Wil had scored and Tom stood on first base. Or rather, he floated slightly above it. The Wildcats had won, 5–4.

It was over. The Big Game was over.

Long live Dillontown.

The team ran out and mobbed Tom. Wil spanked his helmet, knocking it to the ground, laughing and screaming. Tom's mom and dad spun him around. "Amazing!" said his dad.

"We did it, we did it!" cried Rachel, tossing her head back in a circle hug with Frankie, Tara, and Ramón that spun and nearly crushed Tom.

"The HitSim!" said Frankie. "The HitSim!"

"See, it works," said Ramón. "Tom hits 'em where they ain't. And they ain't on the roof!"

Even Del Gato was smiling. He navigated the mob, extending his hand to Tom, saying just two words. *"Gracias, compadre."*

Someone else bumped and spun Tom around, and he caught a glimpse of his parents, surrounded by a mob of reporters. Tom hooted just to hoot.

But when he saw María hobble up, tears streaming, not able to speak, Tom did not know what to do.

Lucky for him, she did. She wobbled right up, bent down,

and bonked her forehead into his. "Nice hit," she said. "Yeah, you really crushed it." And Tom could tell she was only partly joking.

"It was insane!" said Clifford, still wearing his batting gloves. "Did you see it?" he asked anyone who could hear him. "How could they miss that ball?"

"The wind caught it!" said Cody. "It just took off and—and I don't know."

As the celebration began to slow a moment as though to catch its breath, a thought occurred to Tom. "Hey, where's Doc?" he said. He hopped up on his tiptoes, straining to see high into the top row of the stands. But there were too many people in the way for him to see Doc's special spot. "Is he down here?"

As it turned out, all of the questions—from Clifford's about the ball to Tom's about Doc—would be answered, simply enough, by watching replays from several video cameras that had caught the whole scene.

But it was only by viewing one of those tapes, shot from the scoreboard plank, that Tom, and the team, could comprehend the devastating news that hit them that fateful afternoon.

And soon, another, much larger, question would loom. As the crowd joked and jostled and began to make their way down from high in the stands, a cry went up.

"Call 9-1-1!" someone yelled. "Doc's in trouble. Doc's in big trouble."

Doc was dead.

Tom figured it had happened right around the time he'd hit the high pop-up. The stress of the media, the crowd, and the game situation, Tom supposed, along with the pressure Doc'd been under the last few months, had been all too much for his gentle heart.

Pronounced dead before they even carried him out of the bleachers, Doc had once again caused a great stir in Dillontown.

While the hundreds of fans slowly drove off, the media lingered awhile. But none of the players were talking, so they eventually loaded up their gear and headed out for next week's sideshow.

"Are you going to stick around and clean up?" Frankie asked Tom.

Red-eyed and still numb, Tom did not want to go anywhere. "I'm staying. I said I would and I will."

About an hour later, the mayor came ambling through the outfield dust, straight up to Graydog, who was leading one of the cleanup crews. He, Tom, Frankie, Ramón, María, and a few townspeople were quietly raking and bagging trash along the outfield wall.

"Mr. LaRue," the mayor said softly. "I am very, very sorry

to know that Doc is gone." He crossed himself, touching his lip. "He was a very good man. It is unfortunate."

Graydog looked up, but only nodded. He swept at two crumpled paper cups with his rake, sending them flying past his feet.

"And of course," the mayor continued, "congratulations are in order to this miracle team. And what they have accomplished."

Tom and Frankie stopped loading their pile of paper plates, cups, and plastic bags so they could hear better.

"Yeah," said Graydog. "They're good kids."

"I cannot disagree." The mayor lifted his straw cowboy hat and patted his face and neck with a handkerchief. "Well, I see you are busy, so I will not detain you. Except to ask one simple question."

The mayor sidled up a step closer. "As Doc's lawyer, perhaps you can tell me. Did the good doctor leave a will?"

The mayor did not get a simple answer. It was "Yes" and "No."

Yes, Doc had a Last Will and Testament, executed by Grayson LaRue, Esquire, Attorney at Law. That was seven years ago. And Doc had left everything to his only heir, Ken, Jr.—who had died four years ago.

"I see," said the mayor, who thanked Graydog and scurried away.

Tom had a bad feeling about this. "Why'd he ask you that?" he said as he and Frankie rushed up. "That's not good news for the mayor, is it?"

Graydog slammed his rake against the stone wall. "I knew this was coming. He couldn't even wait till the funeral." Graydog's rant caught the attention of Ramón and María as he paced and tossed both hands in the air. "I told Doc over and over again. 'Doc,' I said. 'We've got to sit down and update your will.' But he kept putting it off and putting it off."

Tom closed his eyes at hearing that. So even Doc put things off until it was too late.

"Why?" said María, dragging a bag with her. "What happens now?"

"Well, the property will go into the state probate system, which the courts run. There'll be an estate sale, and the land will go up for auction. Sold to the highest bidder. And I have no doubt who that'll be."

"But Doc told me himself," Tom protested, "that getting involved in the land deal was a mistake. He wished he'd never done it."

"Yeah," said Frankie. "And everyone heard him say that if we won, the town would stay the same."

"That don't mean jack to a beanstalk now," said Graydog. "Because now we're stuck outta luck."

Tom handed Frankie his rake and started walking away. He said nothing. This news, on top of everything else today, was all too much for his not-so-gentle heart. And he just had to walk.

"But we've got witnesses," said María. "That was his intention. That should count for something."

Graydog hung his head. "Sorry, María. Doc's out of the picture now. And at this point, so are we."

The tents had been folded, the cots stashed away. The fire pit reburied, and the Mariachi Marching Band no longer marched or played.

For the last time, the Wildcats hunkered in the bunkhouse. Silent in their grief.

They'd spread out on the wagon-wheel couch or along the pine-plank walls or they lay on their sleeping bags, staring up at the knotty pine beams. And though it was nearly six o'clock on Saturday afternoon, nobody wanted to leave—not yet.

"We won the battle," said Wil, "but we lost the stupid war."

No one responded. Tom's thoughts were on Doc. The funny, eccentric, fiercely independent old coot was the most honest and compassionate man he'd ever met. He thought about the funeral—on Monday, someone said—and how his burial would mark the end of an era.

Then he thought about the chaparral, the Kumeyaay site up on Doc's ridge, and the big-leaf maple trees, all going to the highest bidder.

"When those earthmovers come," he said, "it'll be like they're burying Doc and the whole town in a mass grave."

"I'm going to lay down in front of the first bulldozer I see," said Frankie.

"Me, too," said Cody.

"Won't do any good," Wil told them. "They'll squish your guts and keep on going."

"No, they won't," said Rachel. She and María were lying side by side on their bags, with their bare feet propped against the wall. "They'll just arrest you and throw you in jail."

"You know," said Tara. "I wish Cruz were here. He'd have an idea. How could he just leave? How could he let us down like that?"

Apparently no one felt like answering questions that really had no answers. Except Tom.

"He didn't let us down. He *led* us down. Think about it. From the first time he ran ahead of us down the mountain to taking me to Del Gato's to showing me his pitch to setting up his HitSim game—he was leading us. He showed us how to do the stuff we needed to do."

"Yeah, well, we didn't need this." Wil picked at some white cotton stuffing from a hole in the couch pillow. "First he leaves us with no pitcher, takes our biggest and best bat out of our lineup, and that makes the game so insane that Doc keels over and dies. Cruz was the Death and Doom guy, no doubt, like I thought all along. He spurred Doc's death."

"No, he didn't," said Tom. "That's just an old dumb prophecy, anyway. Cruz was Cruz. That's all he was. Where he is now, who knows? He just—he just cruised on. But he helped us win. He got us to believe in ourselves. He really did a lot."

"Either way," said Clifford. "Doc's dead and he was a great

man, like in the prophecy. And he might've had a great secret. Only problem is, it's too late to help the town now. Dead men tell no tales."

Someone knocked at the door.

"Sorry to interrupt," Mrs. Gallagher called in. She leaned through the open doorway. "We just thought you'd want to know Doc Altenheimer's funeral will be Monday afternoon at Saint Anthony's. The viewing will be from one to three. The memorial begins at four. Jerry and I are handling arrangements and we thought"—she paused a moment, swallowing hard—"it might be nice if one of you would come forward and speak at the service."

She turned and nodded. Del Gato stepped up behind her, then entered the room.

"You all need to know," he began, "you put up one heck of a dog fight." He made sure he connected with any eyes directed his way. "So, I thank you. And, uh, well, I'm taking off." He felt behind him with his black work boot, then took a step back. "So—good-bye."

Tara and Rachel both jumped up, caught him, and hugged him. María limped up right behind. The boys grunted loud "Good-bye"s at their shoes or hands or at the ceiling. Their "Thank you"s started a moment later.

After he left, Mrs. Gallagher said, "Okay, that's all. Thanks for cleaning up around here. Your parents should be along in about half an hour for our Ice Cream Sendoff."

"Oh, good," said Cody. "We're still having it. Clifford, it's all homemade ice cream. We make chocolate and rocky road and everything."

Clifford did not answer. And the silence quickly dampened even Cody's enthusiasm.

"We thought we should keep the tradition alive," Mrs. Gallagher added quietly. "So I'll also need four strong arms to get us started. Say, in about twenty minutes? And Tom, would you and"—she took a step closer to see a face—"and María please go to the chicken coop and get some fresh eggs? We'll need at least a dozen, but collect them all. We haven't been down there in a few days. Thank you." She left.

Tears appeared in Tom's eyes so quickly, they surprised him. Doc had always come down for the ice cream. Tom stood and faced the door so no one would see.

Rachel saved him. "Do you guys think he knew what happened? Do you think he saw, before he died, that we'd won?"

"Oh, yeah," said Frankie. "No doubt." The others agreed.

Tom was hardly listening. As the only one on the team who really knew Doc, Tom was certain he'd be the one to say something at the service on Monday. In front of all those people. Now he missed the old coot more than ever. He'd have known—Doc would have known what to say. Tom would need to sit and ponder, look out the window and dream, before the words came to him. Then he'd practice and practice and still have trouble spitting them out.

But Doc, he always had the right words.

Tom felt as nervous now, walking with María across the back lawn, as he ever had. He could think of nothing clever or impressive or cool to say. And she was looking off to the side, anyway.

"Um, how's your leg?" he blurted out.

"Better than a heart attack," she said. "I'll live."

"Oh." What a dumb question, he told himself. Just walk to the henhouse.

María nudged his arm. "Hey, I think someone wants to see you."

Tom turned and saw Del Gato, out past the workshop, sitting in his battered Apache with the door open. "Tom, got a minute?"

"Yeah." Tom took a step toward him, then stopped and bounced the empty egg basket against his leg. He looked back at María.

She took the basket. "Go, say good-bye. I'll wait."

By the time Tom reached the truck, Del Gato had already pulled the door shut and was facing forward, his elbow on the window frame, his other arm slung over the top of the steering wheel.

"Your mom," he started, "says she told you the story about me finding her in a storm one night."

What a thing to say, thought Tom. "Yeah, wasn't she supposed to?"

"Well, there's more to it." He rolled his shoulders. "I was drunk that night. It was right around the time I realized I'd left baseball for no good reason. I was wandering up in the hills just to drink myself to sleep in some bush or cave or something. But that night, in the middle of the storm, my grandmother, *mi abuelita*, came to me. And told me to follow her."

Del Gato now had both arms draped over the wheel, as if

he had to look through the windshield to see the story he was telling. "But Tom, my grandmother—by then, she'd been dead for twelve years."

Tom's stomach flipped.

Del Gato went on. "But I followed her. She led me to a creek bed where I saw a woman lying in the mud. Cold as ice, but she was still alive. I was too drunk to know what to do, so I just fell on her, covered her with my own body. Figured, at least I'd keep her warm. Maybe an hour or two after that, I woke up. By then the horse'd wandered back. A young gelding."

"Yeah, that's Pronto. That's my horse."

He turned to Tom. "So I loaded up your mom and took her to Doc's."

"You saved her life."

"Well, someone did. I'm not sure it was me."

"Wow," Tom said softly. "Did your *abuelita*—I mean, did you ever see her again?"

He shook his head and reached for the key. "No, only that once. But we'd always had a strong connection. We depended a lot on each other."

The rough-running engine bucked to life. "Here's why I'm bringing this up. Whatever the heck it was I did for your mom that night—and for you and your dad, too, in a way— this week, your family returned the favor." For just the briefest moment, Tom thought he saw a grin break across Del Gato's face. "So thanks for breaking down my wall."

The engine strained a bit, and he drove away.

Slightly dazed, Tom straggled back to where María waited, sitting on the upside-down egg basket.

"What'd he say?"

Tom stared at her as he finished sorting his thoughts. "Not much. He just wanted to say good-bye."

In another minute, Tom and María stood alone in the henhouse with nine watchful chickens clucking around them.

"I didn't know you needed eggs for making ice cream," she said.

"Yeah, for flavor. And they help thicken it up and keep it together."

He set the basket in the center of the coop. Starting at opposite ends, they began checking and gathering from the nesting bins lining the front wall. When they met in the middle, Tom stepped back to the basket and let María check the last one.

"Here," she said. Resting on a knee, María passed him two eggs. Tom took them using both hands, and to do so, he cupped María's hand in his. Even after the delicate eggs were safely in his grasp, she did not pull back.

Her warm, strong, smooth hands lingered in Tom's for an extra instant, a pause he could tell she did on purpose, though she acted as if she were just making sure the eggs were secure.

Then she slid her hands from his, their skin brushing in the motion. Neither Tom nor María dared look at each other.

"That's it," she said. "Got 'em all." She peeked at Tom and smiled. "Let's go."

María rose, turning for the coop door, but Tom said, "Wait."

And she stopped, turned back, and waited.

Now what? thought Tom. What was I thinking?

He looked right at her. María de Lourdes Flores Sanchez, her eyebrows crooked, one high, one low, as if half amused, half annoyed.

Then he grabbed for the one thought, the one he'd been thinking since Thursday, which had been right there a few seconds ago. He knew it had something to do with her face, her mouth, her voice, something. Yes, that was it. The funny things she would say and the looks she would give to go along with them.

"María," he said, "I think you're the most interesting girl I've ever met."

That was it. For the first time in his life, a wild thought had been tracked down through the rough terrain, the canyons and boulders and brush of his brain, right at the moment he needed it. And not only that, he had *spoken* it. Out loud. To a girl.

Her face softened. It melted into perfect symmetry.

"Tom," she said, and that was all she said. Ah, but how she said it. Through a smile. Two syllables, two different notes. Practically a song, a poem, really, that ended with a quick eye-crinkle as an exclamation point.

Well, his brain went blank again. An empty screen, all except for a goofy spaceman screensaver floating across it, shouting, "Don't say another word. Don't say another word."

She pulled open the door for him, and Tom hoisted the

basket full of eggs. But as he started through, this time María said, "Wait."

Tom froze in the doorway, standing on the two-by-four threshold so he could be as tall as possible. She touched his shoulder, cupping it in her hand. "I think you, *Tompadre*, are the bravest boy I will ever know."

Sometime in the dead of night, Tom felt someone shake his shoulder. His eyes blinked open. He looked around. No one there. He propped himself up on an elbow and looked again. His room was empty.

He lay back down, but kept his eyes open.

It was almost a half moon that night, making his bedroom nearly as light as early dawn, though it was just after two.

Tom placed his hands behind his head. He was not going back to sleep. His mind was racing. Why, he wondered, why did Doc have to die right at that moment? With no will? He thought about Cruz, how he came just at the right time and then left—he left through María's dream.

And, oh, yeah, María. He didn't know what to think about María.

Tom sat up and swung his feet to the floor. Gazing out into the backyard, he noticed that it actually felt weird to be sleeping indoors.

He rose and dressed, and without any real plan, he soon found himself outside, crossing the back lawn, under the night calls of mockingbirds and summer wrens in the bottle-brush and pepper trees rimming the grass.

Before long, he was walking through the deserted ballpark, with its still-fresh coat of paint shimmering in moonlight.

"It was right here, folks," he said quietly in his broadcaster's voice, "on this ball field, that Tom 'Crazylegs' Gallagher scrambled his way through a dust storm, through winds gusting up to a hundred miles an hour, to reach first base after hitting a screaming line drive, straight up, dazzling the fielders, a mile high." His voice trailed off. "Folks, you had to have been there."

He knelt with one knee on the ground, crossed his arms over the other. "That was for you, Doc. So long."

Tom looked around at the empty, eerie field. There was one more good-bye still to be said.

"*Adiós*, Cruz de la Cruz," he whispered. "Been good to know you."

Through the moonlight came a hawk screech—the sharp, shrill call of a red-tailed hawk that flew overhead and landed on the dugout roof.

Tom bolted straight up. Adrenaline raced through him as he backed away, eyeballing the tall, square-shouldered bird.

"Cheese, Louise!" He breathed in and out. He blinked to get a better look as the gray-brown hawk roosted, motionless.

In the old days, even yesterday, Tom would've turned that hawk into a story, made him come alive, personified him, and talked to him. "Up pretty early for hunting," he might say. "What, you can't sleep? Join the club."

But he had neither the heart nor the inclination to do that now. Instead he brushed off his knee, turned, and walked back home.

Sitting at the kitchen table, under dim light, Tom opened his Dreamsketcher. He began to draw. Triangles, circles, figure eights. He drew St. Anthony's church. He drew a thousand people in the pews. He drew a coffin. Behind that, he drew himself standing up at the lectern.

It was his way of getting ready for the saddest and scariest day of his life.

He heard someone on the stairs.

"Tom?" his mother whispered. "What are you doing, honey?"

"I can't sleep."

She said nothing at first, *whis-whisp*ing her slippers across the tile to the stove. "Goodness," she said as the burner under the kettle flamed up. "It's not even three o'clock."

"I know, Mom. Which means it's already Sunday morning. And this will be the first Sunday in over two years that I won't—you know, read the box scores—" Tom's breathing grew louder. He placed both elbows on the table and held his head between his fists.

His mother sat down across from him. She watched for a long time.

Tom lowered his arms, rubbed his nose, then resumed work.

He sketched rainfall this time. A mountain rain with wind and fury. Behind the veil of rain he drew an old woman. It was Del Gato's *abuelita*.

"He told me the whole story, Mom. Mr. Del Gato did." Tom paused to let that memory rise up again in his mind. "He said he talked to his grandmother that night, in the middle of the rainstorm."

"Yes, I know."

"That that was how he found you. He followed her."

She only nodded.

"But she was dead."

On a new page, Tom began an outline of Cruz riding into town, crossing the ball field on Screwball. "So he dreamed her up?" he asked. "She wasn't real, so he must have. But how could he dream up someone who had more knowledge than he did?"

"I don't know."

"Know what I just remembered? The word *cruz* means 'cross' in English, doesn't it?"

"Yes, it does."

Tom kept drawing. "So, the name Cruz de la Cruz has two crosses in it." He drew some more. "His name is a double cross." He paused and looked up at her. "And today, we had a double loss. Do you think the prophecy came true?"

"Tom, listen." She rose to catch the teakettle before it whistled. "As far as that prophecy goes, I think it came true when Blackjack Buck died. He came from Yuma, which is east of here. He was a stranger arriving during disastrous times. And there was a double loss of miners and a ball team. And goodness knows how many double crosses. See what I mean? That prophecy's probably come true a hundred times by now."

Tom liked hearing that. He believed in Cruz and he believed in his good heart.

"Who knows, Tom? There's so much we don't understand

or can't explain. But I'll say this. If we die and we don't get to know exactly how the universe really works, I want you to know that I'll feel really cheated."

She drenched the tea bag in her cup. "But I do think Dante's grandmother came to him at the very moment he needed her the most. Don't ask me how or why—I think it was for lots of reasons—but that's my deep-down belief. And that's all I ever thought about it."

Tom set his pencil down. "So, is Doc dead? Or could he come around again—just show up in the middle of a brush-fire or something and save me?"

She laughed. "Maybe. Who can say? But we have our minds and dreams, don't we? We have our memories. We have pictures and letters and things that are passed along to keep people alive for us. And I say that as long as we do, no one really leaves us."

That was exactly what Tom needed to hear. He did have memories of Doc. And pictures. And he even had Doc's notes, his little words of encouragement.

In fact, he decided that those notes would be perfect to include in his eulogy for Doc on Monday.

Mrs. Gallagher rose from the table, taking her cup with her. "I think I might do some reading. Are you going to stay down here and keep drawing?"

Tom nodded. "Till the words come." But now he knew he had his starting point. He flipped to the back of his Dream-sketcher, the very last page. And there, in Doc's perfect hand-writing, Tom found the perfect words.

"Oh, man," he whispered. "Mom."

"What is it?"

He read them again. Doc's great words of encouragement. Boom words, mariachi words, rugged-mountain-man words. And then he laughed.

"What?" his mother repeated. "What are you looking at?"

Tom jumped up, shaking the book. "Dad!" he yelled into the stairwell. "*Wake up*, come down here!"

He bent back the page. "Mom, listen." And he began to read. " 'As of this date, I, Kennesaw Mountain Altenheimer, being of sound and sober mind, do hereby bequeath all of my earthly possessions to my good friend and neighbor, Thomas Gallagher, son of Jerry and Helen Gallagher, of Dillontown, California, to do with as he wishes.' "

The mayor stood alongside his desk, held up Tom's Dreamsketcher, and laughed.

"This is worthless! You expect us to honor a will that's written in the young beneficiary's own diary?"

"It's not a diary!" said Tom, raising his voice as easy as a flag over a ballpark. "And Doc wrote that, not me. Check the handwriting."

Graydog, sitting next to Tom, was already shuffling through his floppy brown valise with the evidence.

"As Doc's lawyer, I can verify his signature and handwriting from all the letters he sent to me over the years. Sorry, Oscar, but this'll stand up in court. There's no doubt Doc wrote this will."

"So what if he did?" came the graggely voice of Alabaster Jones. He sat back in the mayor's high-back office chair and faced the room with a ruby red tip on his smoke-bomb cigar. "There's no witnesses! A will's got to have *two* witnesses. Everybody knows that. That paper's not worth the paper it's—I mean, that paper's not worth a ding dang *diddly-dee*!"

Graydog raised a hand.

"I beg to differ," he offered, calmly. "In the state of California, the law for typed documents is different than for handwritten ones. This will is perfectly legal, and it does *not* need witnesses." He rose and retrieved Tom's Dreamsketcher from the mayor and held it aloft. "This paper is worth more than you are, Mr. Jones."

And so it was.

Tom Gallagher was now a millionaire. Not $6 million, but about $1.5 million—the value of Doc's house and land as agricultural property. And that suited Tom just fine.

Tom felt so good, in fact, that he graciously invited his whole family to live with him in his new home, which was bigger and finer than their own and with a much nicer view.

His father said they could rent out their old farmhouse, and the income would not only cover a loan to pay any taxes due, but it would provide them with an extra three hundred dollars a month to boot.

But the best news was that Graydog and Tom had already discussed filing for an official patent on Tom's version of the HitSim game. And he would need it. The news reports about the library batting practice sessions and the effect they had in such a short time had inquiries flying through cyberspace by the hundreds already. They came from everywhere, moms, dads, Little Leagues and colleges—even a couple pro teams!

"I might have to employ a few people," said Tom.

In a town where the discovery of gold was once an everyday occurrence, Tom Gallagher realized he had found something far more valuable. He had found one of the great secrets of the universe. His voice. Not his singing voice or his writing voice, but his real voice. The out-loud one. And the courage to use it—before it was too late.

That afternoon, Tom climbed up into the hayloft over the barn. He sat in the loading door with his boots dangling and a brand-new Dreamsketcher on his lap. He looked south, way off to the hills of Mexico.

And he began to write.

People down in Dillontown, he started, *don't agree on much.* He looked up, this time to the east. He studied the ridge crest, as if at any moment he would see a horse and rider. Then he wrote some more.

Not the skateboard laws. Not the billboard laws. The economy. The ecology. There's days when they don't even agree on which way the wind is blowing.

But they agree on this. If there never was a boy named Cruz de la Cruz, somebody would've come along and invented him.

Literature Circle Questions

Use these questions and the activities that follow to get more out of the experience of reading *The Boy Who Saved Baseball* by John H. Ritter.

1. How is Doc Altenheimer going to decide whether to sell his property to developers?

2. Dante Del Gato has long been a fascinating but mysterious person to Tom. Who is Del Gato, and why is Tom so interested in him?

3. Why are the people of Dillontown so eager to see the outcome of the game? And why do so many reporters, photographers, and television crews, including some from ESPN, come to watch the big game?

4. Tall tales fill this story. What is it about Cody's story concerning Del Gato's electric fence that doesn't make sense? Can you come up with any other examples of "stretching the truth" in this novel?

5. What does "earthen knowledge" mean? What about a "starborne hunch?" How do hunches and knowledge contribute to Tom's character? Cruz's character? Del Gato's character? The outcome of the novel?

6. Do any members of the Wildcats remind you of anyone you know? Which of the Wildcats—besides Tom—do you like the best?

7. In the beginning of the story, Tom struggles with feeling confident, especially when playing baseball or talking to others. What advice would you give to Tom to help him with these struggles?

8. Evaluate the handling of the game of baseball in this book. Is there a culture of baseball? If so, does it have its own separate social rules, vocabulary, and value system? How would you describe it?

9. What do you think the title of this book means? Who is "the boy who saved baseball," and how do you know?

10. What are some of the lessons that Tom learns over the course of this book—about baseball, about himself, about life?

11. What kind of person does Dante Del Gato turn out to be in the end? Does he change over the course of the story, or does Tom just begin to know him better?

12. How would you define the word "hero?" Is a person a hero if no one knows or witnesses what the person did? Have you ever thought someone was called a hero without justification? What part does the person's motivation (or hidden agenda) play in determining whether he or she is actually a hero?

13. The author writes, "A boy kept distant from the earth is a boy dissatisfied." How does this philosophy play out in the novel? Find physical, concrete signs of it as well as mental ones. To what extent does Tom come to see this to be true?

14. After saving the town of Dillontown, inheriting Doc Altenheimer's fortune, and beginning a business with HitSim, Tom Gallagher's life is about to change. Imagine what Tom's life will be like ten or twenty years into the future. How has he handled his success and his wealth? Is he playing baseball? Has he kept his friends from the Wildcats? Is he still writing in his Dreamsketcher?

15. In the baseball lexicon, a substitute or "relief" pitcher—such as Tom in the Big Game—may get credit for a win, a loss, or a save. Make an argument supporting the idea that in this story, Tom seems to have done all three. What did Tom win, what did he lose, and what did he save?

Note: These literature circle questions are keyed to Bloom's taxonomy as follows: Knowledge: 1–3; Comprehension: 4–5; Application: 6–8; Analysis: 9–10; Synthesis: 11–12; Evaluation: 13–15.

Activities:

1. Make a set of baseball cards—one for each member of the Wildcats' team. On each card include a drawing of the character as you imagine him or her. Instead of listing statistics for each player, describe each player's strengths on the team as well as important personality traits.

2. What do you think the front page of the Dillontown newspaper looked like the day after the big game? Write newspaper-style articles telling the story of the big game, Doc Altenheimer's death, and the town's reaction to both. Use headlines and photos to make your articles look like a real newspaper.

3. Imagine that a few days after the big game Tom receives a letter from Cruz de la Cruz. What does the letter say? How does Cruz explain his absence from the game? How does he feel about the Wildcats and their win?

Other Books by this Author:
Choosing Up Sides, Philomel, 1998
Over the Wall, Philomel, 2000

Please visit the author's Web site for further questions, lesson plans, and activities: www.johnhritter.com Look for an especially recommended activity on "neologism," the art of creating new words.